BLOOD BOND

Cora's Choice – Book 5

V. M. BLACK

Aethereal Bonds
aetherealbonds.com

Swift River Media Group
Washington, D.C.

ISBN-13: 978-1501037184
ISBN-10: 1501037188

FICTION / General
FICTION / Coming of Age
FICTION / Fantasy / Urban
FICTION / Gothic
FICTION / Political
FICTION / Romance / General
FICTION / Romance / New Adult
FICTION / Romance / Paranormal
FICTION / Thrillers / Supernatural
FICTION / Thrillers / Political

THE VAMPIRE'S KISS

I SWALLOWED, CLOSING MY EYES, feeling the expectation twisting tighter and tighter inside me. I was going to do this thing again, knowing what was coming. I remembered the insanity of that first night, the madness and the pain and the ecstasy, the glory and terror all flowing together until I didn't know where one stopped and another began.

It really was going to happen. Again. Tonight.

"Then show me," I said, opening my eyes and meeting his gaze. My vampire. There was nothing human about him now. And somehow, it made me want him more.

Desire flared deep in his eyes.

"Your arm," he said, and he held out his hand.

I unbuckled then and turned in my seat, putting my hand in his. My insides shivered a little at the contact, my skin flushing. He pushed my sleeve up my arm, and I was reminded of our first encounter, when he had drawn my blood.

"You're willing?" he asked, looking at me with those haunted eyes.

"Yes," I breathed. "You know I am."

Aethereal Bonds

aetherealbonds.com

Cora's Choice

The Alpha's Captive

Acknowledgements

To Brandie and Emily, my first readers.

CONTENTS

CHAPTER ONE

The bond could be broken.

I stood on the sidewalk in front of the bookstore, my phone digging into my palm as I grappled with the bombshell that Cosimo had just dropped into my life.

Free. Could I really believe that I could ever be free again?

I didn't dare trust anything Cosimo said. I needed to be certain. Looking down at my phone, I realized that confirmation was just a call away. My hands shook as I pulled up the list of contacts. At the very top of my favorites, there it was:

"<3 Clarissa."

I couldn't guess why she'd added her number. A

joke? A kind of winking reference to her role in getting my phone back? When I'd first seen her entry, I couldn't imagine a situation in which I'd choose to dial her up. Clarissa might look young enough to fit in with my friends, but what kind of casual chat could I have with a creature who was probably five times as old as my Gramma and killed humans like me for their blood?

Or at least, humans like I used to be....

Now I gave a silent thanks for whatever whim had caused her to add herself to my phone, and I punched through the menu to call her.

For just a moment, I thought about what a ludicrous scene I presented—a college student, her backpack over one shoulder, standing on the sidewalk and dialing the number of a monster out of myth.

But a lot of things about my life had been ludicrous recently. This didn't even make the top ten.

The phone rang—once, twice, three times. My heart had begun to sink when Clarissa's musical voice suddenly answered, suppressed laughter in it.

"Cora! I didn't think you'd really call. Do you feel like doing something outrageously girly? How about a spa day? I haven't had one of those in an age, but we'd have to skip the tanning bed, if that used to be your thing."

Yeah, it was Clarissa, all right. I thought out how to approach her so that she wouldn't instantly call up Dorian and tell him what I was up to. She liked to give the impression of being flighty, but I was pretty sure that she was whip-smart underneath all the show. I needed her to confirm Cosimo's story without raising

2

any suspicions. And if what Cosimo told me was true, that would be tricky because it meant that Dorian had been deliberately hiding information about the bond that tied me to him.

"Sorry, Clarissa. I'm going to meet my boyfriend this afternoon," I said. Geoff and I had never actually made it to a formal relationship, but I'd promised that we would if the leukemia treatment worked. Since I was now cancer-free, I figured it was close enough to true.

"Oh," the vampire—the agnate—said, abruptly serious. "That's really not a good idea."

"Well, Dorian did say that he wasn't going to force me to give up my old life," I pressed on. "And my boyfriend's part of that. On the other hand, Dorian did make rather…specific claims about my person."

That I was his, forever, body, blood, and soul.

"I think a boyfriend is definitely out of the question now," Clarissa said, unusually serious. "You really don't want to be even thinking about that."

But she still hadn't said why. Why did she have to clam up now, of all times?

"Well, that's why I wanted to talk to you," I said. "I don't want to hurt Dorian's feelings or anything, but you know, I saw an agnate at the party two nights ago who had two cognates, so I figured it might be okay."

"It's one thing for an agnate to have two cognates. But a cognate simply can't have another relationship." Clarissa's voice betrayed her alarm.

"I understand if it's just not been done before, but I figured that Dorian wouldn't be such a prude," I babbled, pressing onward.

"Doesn't have anything to do with being a prude or not," Clarissa said. "A cognate who has slept with another human wouldn't be a cognate anymore."

I rocked on my feet, a burst of something— elation? terror?—going through me.

It was true, it was true, it was true....

I had a choice. I could be free.

"What do you mean?" I asked, trying not to give anything away in my voice.

Clarissa's horror came clearly through the phone. "Look, you only get one shot at being a cognate. Once you're converted, that's it. You're bound to that agnate and none other. If another agnate comes and tries to drink from you, you'll both die. And if you sleep with another human man, you'll stop being a cognate. You'll start aging again, and you can get sick, and eventually, you'll die. And there's no going back because then you'd be poison to every agnate. Even Dorian."

"So it's permanent," I said. I had to be absolutely sure. My future was riding on it. "Once you've turned back human, you can't ever become a cognate again."

"Absolutely," she said. "Stay away from that guy. Whatever he was to you, he's not your boyfriend anymore. Even if you don't mean to, if it goes wrong, you'll lose everything, Cora."

I'd lose everything except for the life I'd originally wanted to save.

"That's awful." I hoped I sounded like I meant it, because I had no idea yet what I thought. "Thanks for telling me. I didn't want to bother Dorian with it because, well, I wasn't fully sure how he'd take it." No kidding. "But now that I know, I'll steer clear of trouble."

"Give it a year or so and you won't even have to worry about it," Clarissa said, cheerful again. "You'll be strong enough by that point that no mere human—or two or three, even—could overpower you if they wanted to. Of course, you'll never be anything like as strong as us agnates, but at least you won't have to worry about humans anymore."

That was another revelation. What more would change, given enough time?

"Thanks," I said. There was nothing else to say. "I guess I'll see you at Dorian's New Year's Eve party?"

"Possibly," Clarissa said breezily. "You never can tell, with Dorian."

No, you couldn't.

"Bye, then," I said.

"Goodbye."

I hung up.

I could be free....

I tried to savor the thought of it, but my head was filled with shadows of Dorian. His rare, true smile, the phantom of his hands on my shoulders, my face, my breasts, the memory of his mouth on mine and the words that he murmured in my ear.... All echoes of the bond that bent my will to his desires, that narrowed my future to the path that had been laid out for his cognates since long before I was born.

I could get rid of it now—break it once and for all. And the memories and shadows would be gone, I was sure, along with the craving that gnawed at my very bones.

I was sure.

I had to be.

Taking a deep breath, I headed for my car. If I left now, I'd get to the Mall at Columbia only a few minutes after I'd agreed to meet Geoff and my best friend Lisette. And then I could let things play out as they would.

Ever since my cancer diagnosis three months ago, my life had turned into a narrow corridor with nothing but dead ends at the turnings. I could choose to try an aggressive drug therapy—or I could die. When that failed, I could agree to Dorian Thorne's dangerous, experimental treatment—or give up on my life. Everything was posed as a choice, but there really had been no choice at all.

Now, for the first time in months, I had one.

I turned the key in my Ford Focus. It growled temperamentally to life, nothing at all like the honey-smooth hum of Dorian's cars. I backed out of the parking space and turned onto the street, heading for the Beltway.

I had gone to Dorian's house a willing subject for his experimental research. I had no way of knowing then his real purpose, which was to identify the humans most likely to be turned into cognates by a vampire's kiss rather than dying as most did. The cancer cure that I was seeking was nothing more than a side effect of that change, of the bond that now tied me to him and gave him power over my mind.

I had already learned that he would change me consciously if it was important enough to him. And I knew that he changed me unconsciously, subtly but inevitably, every time I was with him.

I bit my lip as I took the exit for the Columbia mall.

For now, I still had enough of my will left that I could make a choice. Soon, I feared, all that would be gone.

Because I wanted him, even now. I wanted him and missed him like I imagined an amputee missed a limb—an aching absence that was as much a part of me as anything else.

Time was running out.

The mall was swamped with the post-Christmas shopping crush. I had to park far out from the entrance to Marble Slab, where we'd agreed to meet. I locked the car and zipped up my coat, settling my sunglasses more firmly over my eyes as I headed toward the ice cream shop, my head down against the stiff wind.

"Cora!"

Lisette's squeal made me look up. She was running toward me, a huge grin on her face. And behind her, at a more restrained pace, came Geoff.

Chapter Two

"Hey, guys," I called back. "You could have waited inside."

"We were," Geoff assured me. "Lisette saw you from inside and had to run out."

Lisette flung her arms around me in a soft, warm embrace, and I hugged her back, hard. It seemed like forever since I had seen the two of them, but it had really only been a week and a half, and I'd been unconscious for five days of that.

I looked at Geoff. He had a slightly goofy, slightly shy grin on his face.

It sure didn't take long to turn my life upside down, I thought. But maybe I could still put it right side up again.

"So, you're really better?" Lisette demanded.

"I checked my lab results this morning, and my lymphocytes are down to 15,000," I said.

"That's good?" she prompted.

"Well, they were at 200,000, so yeah," I said.

Lisette squeezed me again.

"That's great," Geoff said. "Do I get a hug, too?"

"Of course," I said. I disengaged myself from Lisette and gave him a quick, one-handed squeeze, ignoring the jolt that went through me—guilt at betraying Dorian, but also a sudden, desperate relief at how warm and strong and human he felt.

Geoff and I had started a relationship long before Dorian had entered the picture, I reminded myself. If anyone had been betrayed, it was him.

"Let's get inside," said Geoff.

He hooked an arm around my waist and the other around Lisette's shoulders and started herding us into the mall entrance. I welcomed the trickle of self-consciousness that made me look straight ahead at his touch, too studied to be as casual as he pretended. Whatever else Dorian had done to me, he hadn't killed what I felt for Geoff.

And I began to truly believe that I might be free.

"I've got to get a couple of pairs of jeans," Lisette said as we stepped through the double doors. The mall was still decked out in all its Christmas glory. "And some business clothes because I've got that receptionist gig at my uncle's law firm in the spring."

"Nepotism," I grumbled good-naturedly.

"Yep," she said smugly. She led us quickly past the

storefronts.

"Got any other openings?" I asked.

"Filing clerk," she said. "But really, that's half scanning. They've got a stuffed file room, and they're trying to digitize everything."

That seemed like a possibility. "Think you could score me an interview?"

"Sure thing," she said. "Pay's good for the work. Like twelve dollars an hour."

"Is that regular pay or niece pay?" I joked.

She stuck her tongue out at me. "Niece pay is fifteen an hour."

"So, who's footing the bill for the clothes?" I asked.

She grinned. "Daddy, of course. He gave me a five hundred dollar cash card—for incidentals, he said. I still had enough from my job last summer to cover my books, so it's time for a shopping spree."

"Three hours from now, you're going to regret agreeing to this," I predicted, looking up at Geoff. He'd let go of Lisette, but his arm was still around my waist. It felt right. It felt good.

But not as good as Dorian, part of my brain thought. I shut it out.

"I doubt it," he said, smiling down at me.

I ducked my head to hide the blush I felt creeping up my cheeks. "We'll see."

Lisette chattered on, pretending to be oblivious as we were dragged along in her wake.

"Let's start here," she announced. She led us through the wide opening in the Macy's mall storefront and headed straight for the business clothes. I helped her pick out a few likely-looking blouses, and she pawed through racks of nearly-identical skirts, making gleeful noises at some and turning up her nose in contempt at others.

"You can probably wear pants, you know," I pointed out. "It's not the nineteen-fifties."

"Then who will look at my legs?" Lisette demanded.

"Are you trying to snag yourself a full partner, Lisette Bonner?" I demanded.

Lisette had curves, and she knew how to dress them. Even when she didn't seek out male attention, she never seemed to lack it. She rode the edge of the top end of the misses section, and she freely admitted that the lack of fashion choices in the plus sizes was the single greatest contributing factor to her plateauing weight.

"Nah," she said. "They're all too old. Maybe a junior partner. I'll have law school homework next year, and neither one of you two are going to be there to help me out."

"You don't need any help," I said. "I'm like your security blanket. You study just fine on your own."

"Don't spoil her fun," Geoff said.

Once Lisette had grabbed so much clothing that the hangers covered one arm from elbow to wrist, she said, "You guys might as well wait out in the mall. This is going to take a while."

I lifted an eyebrow because I'd never known Lisette to miss a chance to haul me into the dressing room to confirm her strong—and excellent—opinions about each piece of clothing she was considering.

She just looked back with an expression of innocence that I did not buy for a single moment.

"Sure, Lisette," I said. "I'm sure you'll be able to find us."

"What else are cell phones for?" she asked, heading toward the dressing room.

I shook my head at her back.

"Well?" Geoff prompted.

"Let's find somewhere to sit, then," I said.

Geoff offered his hand. I took it. His palm was warm and rough from his lacrosse calluses. How different his grasp was from Dorian's cool, smoother one. I knew who Geoff was in a way that I could never know Dorian, and when he smiled, I felt only the flush of his attention and not any of the conflicted, fearful thoughts that the vampire stirred in my heart.

We headed out into the main part of the mall again, where a thousand conversations echoed against the hard floor and high walls, swallowing us comfortably in the din and bustle.

"I've got to hit up Auntie Anne's," I said. "I skipped lunch."

Geoff frowned. "That's not smart."

I knew what he meant. I was still too thin. "It wasn't planned, believe me. Something just came up." Yeah, Cosimo the vampire had come up in a luxury car and whisked me away to a supernatural dive bar.

We checked the nearest map kiosk and started off, still hand in hand through the crush of shoppers. Santa was gone from his wonderland, but Christmas scenes still cluttered the main walkways and wreaths and garlands festooned the walls.

"I got an acceptance yesterday," I said suddenly, without planning to.

Geoff's expression got very still, his hand tightening fractionally around mine. "Where to?"

"University of Chicago," I said.

His broad face split into a grin. "Your top pick."

"Close to yours, too," I prompted.

"Yeah. Chicago, Berkley, and Harvard. And I just got my rejection from Harvard."

"So you're in at two," I said.

"Yep. It's going to be either Chicago or Berkley," he agreed.

"When do you decide?"

"Deadline's in May, after the fellowships and assistantship offers go out."

"Plenty of time, then." Plenty of time to find out exactly how serious we were going to be.

"Plenty," he agreed.

We reached the back of the line at Auntie Anne's. I got three sesame pretzels and a Coke, pulling my hand reluctantly out of Geoff's to take my food. I wolfed down the food as we headed back toward Macy's. Geoff waved me over to an empty bench close to the store.

"So, you really are recovering," Geoff said as I shoved the last wax paper wrapper back into the bag. "You already look a ton better."

"What's that supposed to mean?" I demanded with pretend outrage, setting my drink at my feet.

Playing along, he held up his free hand as if to ward me off. "Hey, hey! You know what I meant."

I laughed. Geoff was always good at making me laugh.

"Anyhow, it's good," Geoff said.

"Yeah, it is."

There must have been some unintentional sarcasm in my response because Geoff frowned at me and caught my free hand in his. "I really mean it, Cora. I'm glad you're getting better—more glad than I can say. More glad than I probably have any right to be."

"What do you mean by that?" I asked, struck by the peculiarity of his phrasing.

"You've been a good friend. A really good friend for three years now. But I think I've made it pretty clear that I want you to be more than that. And to be honest, I already consider you to be more than that."

His eyes were unusually serious, their puppy dog liquidity as charming as it ever had been. I dropped my gaze to our entwined hands. His skin was golden against mine, golden, warm, and entirely human. I turned my wrist slightly so I couldn't see the bond-mark on it.

I had a choice. I had chosen life. Now I could choose which life it was that I wanted.

"I feel the same," I said.

He treated me to a boyish smile. "Good. 'Cause I just kinda put myself out there just now. And it would have been pretty awkward if we'd had to sit here for the next half hour while Lisette was pretending not to be giving us time apart if you'd shot me down."

"Our goodbye didn't convince you of that?" I returned.

He laughed, a bright sound. Geoff was, I thought, exactly what he appeared. Simple, direct, uncomplicated. As smart as hell, of course, for all his casual approachability. But he was day to Dorian's night, a world away from angst and moral complexities.

"Well, I did sort of initiate that," he said. "Maybe you were just being polite."

"Polite?" I demanded. I punched him in the arm with my free hand. "Polite stops with me long before your tongue is in my mouth."

His laughter stopped abruptly, and he gave me a look that I knew too well.

"Here?" I said. But my breath was already coming a bit fast.

"Why not?" he asked.

"Maybe because we're in a mall," I said. "With thousands of after-Christmas shoppers all around."

"You aren't ashamed of me, are you?" he asked.

"Of course not," I said. "I'm just not that into PDA."

"Just a peck, then," he said virtuously. "On the cheek."

"All right," I agreed, smiling despite myself.

He bent forward. I felt his breath on my cheek. I couldn't help it. I turned into the kiss, catching his mouth full-on. His lips were hot against mine and tasted like mint toothpaste. My heart sped up, my belly growing pleasantly warm and my head light by the time we broke off.

It wasn't like Dorian's kiss. Nothing at all. It wasn't

deep enough to lose myself inside. But it was still sweet, sweet and true.

In Dorian's world, I never knew what was true and what was delusion.

He smiled at me, and I smiled back ruefully.

"Cheek, huh?" he said.

"It's close enough, isn't it?" I said.

"Regrets?" he asked.

If he only knew....

I shook my head. "Not about this."

"So," he said, "about the whole 'next semester' thing. Mind if we get a bit of a jump on that?"

"I think we just did," I said.

"Want to go out, I mean? We could go to the National Harbor for New Year's Eve."

I felt a pang of guilt. "Sorry. I already promised a friend I'd go to a party with him."

"Him?" The pronoun did not go unnoticed. "Anyone I know?"

"No," I said evasively. "Just somebody I know from the clinic."

"How about tonight, then?" he asked lightly, utterly secure in his knowledge of my attraction to him. Secure in his trust of me. "Better get a jump on that *him*. Dinner and a movie?"

"Sounds good. Let's see what there is."

I freed my hand to use my cell phone, flipping through the movie listings.

"I don't do chick flicks," I warned him. "So if you want to see the newest Jennifer Lopez whatever, you'll have to take Lisette."

"What if they were showing *The Princess Bride?*" he challenged.

"*The Princess Bride* is not a chick flick," I said frostily. "It's a classic. And if you don't know that, then we definitely shouldn't be going out at all."

He chuckled and snagged the phone out of my hands. "Okay, what do you want to see? Explosions and chases? Or superheroes?"

"Don't superheroes come with explosions and chases?" I countered. "If I have to pick…eh, let's skip the comic book one. Sarah will probably want to drag us all to watch it later. She's kind of crazy about those."

"All right, then. Arundel Mills, eight p.m. showing, and I'll pick you up at six-thirty?" he asked.

"Ooo, like a real date," I said.

"It is a real date." He made a face at me. "It'd better be, or I'm downgrading you to McDonald's and a matinee."

I laughed. "Yeah, it's a real date."

Lisette came into view with a garment bag over her arm. "One hundred fifty dollars down! One hundred to go," she announced as she drew near. Her eyes burned with curiosity, but she pretended that she was thinking of nothing but her clothes.

"Saving a bit for the school year, are you?" I said.

"Well, everyone needs pizza money, right?" She grinned. "You two ready to go?"

"Sure," I said.

Geoff stood up, and I grabbed my phone back and pushed to my feet.

"Nordstrom's next." Lisette gave me a broad wink

and strode off, leaving us to follow as we would.

Geoff extended his hand again, and I took it, glad for its warmth.

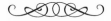

CHAPTER THREE

"That was good," I said four hours later, zipping my jacket up to my chin as I shivered.

We stood outside The Cheesecake Factory, a short walk from the Arundel Mills theater. I'd expected some level of awkwardness at dinner—it was only our second attempt at something resembling a real date, after all. But everything had been easy and natural, the way it always was with Geoff.

The way it never was with Dorian.

I pushed that thought out of my head.

Geoff playfully tugged my hood up over my head. "We can wait inside the mall until it's time to go inside the theater."

"Nah. Let's walk," I said. "It's quieter out here."

I took his offered hand.

"Your hands are always so cold," he observed.

"Maybe yours are just warm," I countered.

He shoved our clasped hands into his coat pocket. "There," he said. "Now they'll both be warm."

I put my free hand into my other pocket. Together, we ambled across the parking lot toward the theater entrance. There were a couple of small, dirty piles of snow where the snowplow had pushed them, melting slowly on the islands of grass, but the rest of the parking lot was bare and dry.

Reflexively, I scanned the windswept expanse. I didn't know what I was looking for—another assassin, Cosimo, or maybe Dorian himself. But there was no one in sight except a mother pushing a stroller one-handed as she held tight to a toddler with her other hand.

Everything was perfectly, completely normal.

"So, your windsurfing story," I said, picking up the thread of conversation that had been dropped when we'd wrestled with our coats outside the restaurant.

He grinned at me. "Okay, so Dale and I were out a few hundred yards from shore when we hit this patch of jellyfish. You've seen a jelly or two washed up on the shore before—but nothing like this. I mean, they were everywhere, and you could feel it when the finbox hit them. You have to remember that these boards were like twenty or thirty years old—something Dale's dad had gotten as a teenager that lived in their garage. They were cheap to begin with, cheap and battered, way worse than any of the stuff you find at the rental places at the beach. But they were free."

"Sounds like a start to a really great day," I said. It felt so good, walking side-by-side with Geoff, our shoulders rubbing as we stepped. I clung onto the sensation, writing it into my brain with the fervency of someone who was afraid of losing it all.

"No kidding. So here we were, plowing through this raft of jellies, Dale wearing nothing but board shorts. Our boards shook a little every time we sliced through one. And all that shaking loosened Dale's mast from its base, and as it flew off, so did he."

"Oh, no," I said.

"Oh, yes. I'd been wondering if those were stinging jellyfish. I found out about half a second after Dale hit the water. He started screaming and thrashing, struggling to get his board back together. I wasn't as good at windsurfing as he was, so it took me a while to circle back to him, and by the time I got there, he had his mast back in its base and was back on the board after a waterstart, still cursing."

"Crap," I said.

"When I got close enough, I could hear what he was saying. 'They stung me in the mouth! The freaking mouth!'"

I groaned.

"Anyhow, we went straight back to shore, and after a visit to the hospital, Dale spent the rest of the weekend watching TV and slathering on the medicated cream he got. And I never went out again without a long-sleeved rashguard."

"I can imagine," I said. "Wasn't much of a Memorial Day weekend, was it?"

"Well, it was memorable," Geoff said, waggling his eyebrows to let me know the pun was deliberate.

I jostled him deliberately with my shoulder, and we kept walking.

"So, this friend of yours, the guy from the clinic," Geoff began. "What does he look like?"

My chest tightened, and I felt suddenly colder.

"Why?" I asked, trying to keep my voice light. "Jealous?"

"I was just asking because I wondered if he was the same guy I met while I was waiting for you to come downstairs tonight."

I fought down a wave of panic. Clarissa could have told Dorian, and if he knew about Geoff, he'd never let me go. He couldn't afford to, could he? He'd come and he'd get me and I wouldn't come out of his mausoleum of a house again until I was truly and utterly his.

And how far away was that point now, really?

"Tallish," I said around the strangling tightness in my throat. "Black hair. Blue eyes."

"Oh," he said. "I guess it's not him, then."

Not him. Not Dorian, come to stop me.

My hand had tightened around Geoff's, and I forced it to relax. "Why do you think he had anything to do with me?"

"Because he came up to my car and knocked on my window. When I rolled it down, he said, 'Waiting for Cora?' That kind of gave me the hint."

Not Dorian—but who, then?

"What did you say?" I asked.

"I said, 'Maybe.' Kind of a dumb answer, but I was

so surprised, I didn't really know what to say."

"And what did he say?"

"'You'll be good for her.' Just like that. Then, 'See that you treat her right.' And then he was gone."

Not someone Geoff knew, so almost certainly from Dorian's world—and only one other agnatic man had been lurking about, one who would be happy that I'd have a human date.

I asked, "Was he a little shorter than you? Light brown hair, sunglasses, brown leather blazer, a D&G t-shirt?"

"Yeah, that was him," Geoff said. "Well, I don't really know how tall he was because I was sitting in the car, but that seemed to be him."

"That's Cosimo," I said. "*Not* my friend. But I met him at the clinic, too."

"Is there something I should know about him?" Geoff looked grave. "Like, is he stalking you?"

"I don't know. I don't think so. He showed up to-day on campus, wanting to talk to me. He's overly interested in my love life, but I think mainly it isn't that he wants to date me but that he doesn't want my—my friend to," I finished a bit lamely. I had almost called Dorian my agnate. That would have required a bit of explanation that I wasn't ready to give.

"But he isn't," Geoff said. "Dating you, I mean."

I closed my eyes for a second, and all the sensa-tions washed over me, Dorian holding me, kissing me, his mouth and hands all over me....

"No, not dating," I said aloud. What we had could not be encompassed by that word.

"So you think this Cosimo guy will go away on his own? Or do you need to do something about him?"

I looked up at him. He held none of Dorian's power, but also none of Dorian's terror over me. He was handsome, kind, and so completely human. He was everything I'd wanted and the way back to my old life, the one I'd planned out so carefully. The one my Gramma knew.

"I think he'll go," I said.

We'd passed the theater entrance some time before. Geoff pulled his phone from his pocket and frowned at it. "Twenty minutes until the show, now," he said. "Might as well head in."

"Yeah," I agreed.

And we did.

We got drinks and popcorn and jammed our jackets under our seats in the half-empty theater. While the previews were still running, Geoff smiled at me and wrapped his arm around my shoulders, and I snuggled into him. He smelled of soap, deodorant, and body spray, a pleasant combination, and his chest was warm and firm.

The movie was the third installment in a blockbuster action series, which meant more camera shaking, more violence, and even less plot. It was mindless fun. I ran out of my popcorn first, and Geoff playfully popped a kernel of his into my mouth, his fingers brushing my lips.

I looked up at him.

"Still hungry, are you?" he asked, leaning close enough that none of the people around us could hear.

"I'm still catching up," I said. "Putting some meat on these bones."

"I like you the way you are now," Geoff said. He grinned. "Of course, I liked you the way you were before you got sick, too."

He leaned down, pulling me to him against the arm of the chair between us, his mouth finding mine. It was hot, so hot against mine, and it tasted of Coke and popcorn and him. I leaned into it, kissing him back, trying to push from my mind the memory of another mouth, other kisses that roused in me the kinds of sensations that I knew Geoff never could.

He broke off suddenly as his tray with his popcorn and drink started to slide off his lap, catching it right before it went over.

He laughed, and I did, too.

"Well, that never happens in the movies," he said.

"No, no it doesn't," I agreed.

After the movie was over, we walked side-by-side to his car. His hand held mine firmly. He hit the unlock button on his key fob and walked me to the passenger side.

"Oh, chivalrous," I joked. "Are you going to open it, too?"

"Sure," he said. "But first, I was planning on this."

He turned so we were face-to-face. Taking both my hands, he leaned down and kissed me. I leaned back against the cold metal door, opening to him, glad for his heat, his humanity. Eventually, I pulled back, catching my breath, and he kissed my cheek, my neck. My heart beat faster, my skin flushing even in the cold. And for a moment, just one moment, he was the only man in the world.

A mall security truck rolled by slowly, the guard glaring at us suspiciously from inside.

"We'd better go," I said. "Or that guy's going to kick us out."

Geoff straightened. "Your apartment?"

I knew what he was asking—both things. I nodded, not trusting myself to speak.

He opened the car door for me, and I got in. He joined me, going to the driver's side. He shoved the keys in the ignition, then grabbed my face in his hands and kissed me again for a very long time.

I didn't want it to end. I didn't want to think. I didn't want to let anything else in my brain except his touch, his mouth, his hands—I didn't want to let the darkness back in.

Finally, he started the car. The headlights flicked on, and he backed out of the parking space.

"Well," I said.

"Well," he echoed.

I knotted my hands in my lap, watching his profile as he drove. Was this what I wanted? Was Geoff what I wanted?

He was everything that I had wanted, before. I knew that much. Until little more than a month ago, when I had walked into Dorian Thorne's office, and he had pierced me with those eyes, touched me with his hands....

Geoff's hand slid from the steering wheel to cover mine. I clasped it.

Geoff was real. He was human. He could never make me want to give him a part of myself that I did not choose to. He couldn't fill my mind with heady madness, set my entire body to singing at his touch—

But my blood still heated with Geoff, and he would never take away the life I'd worked so hard to save. That was the life that he belonged to—grad school, job, house, family. He slotted so nicely into that progression. He'd never make me want to give it all up. He'd never twist me into something else, someone else.

I squeezed Geoff's hand and watched the cars go by.

When we got out at the parking lot nearest my apartment, I looked around surreptitiously with a sudden uneasiness that Cosimo would pop up again—that Dorian would step from the shadows and call my name and I would have no choice but to come into his arms. But there was no sign of either of them.

"Looks like your stalker's disappeared," Geoff said.

"Don't say that," I protested. "It's not even funny to joke about."

"You're right. It isn't." He kissed my cheek. "Forgive me?"

I rolled my eyes at him but smiled. "Of course."

I swiped my card to get us into the building. Geoff looped his arms around my waist in the elevator and kissed my neck. I unlocked my apartment door and muttered, "One moment," and ducked into the bathroom, locking the door behind me. After washing my hands, I brushed my teeth and splashed water on my face. The teardrop ruby necklace, Dorian's gift, winked up at me from the counter where I had left it before our date. It hadn't seemed right to wear it.

I felt him. Dorian. I felt him all around me, the memory of his touch, his look, the shadow of his presence. I couldn't escape it.

Except maybe I could.

I stared at myself in the mirror. My hair was a little tousled, my eyes unnaturally bright. Did I want to? Did I really want to give him up forever? He offered fabulous wealth, near immortality. The chance to feed a country, maybe. Surely what he was asking was cheap in return.

Especially since I would give it to him again for absolutely nothing except for what he did to me—and the light in his eyes when he looked at me, a light that couldn't be love but might be something very close.

I took a deep, shuddering breath. That wasn't me. It couldn't be me. It was the bond talking, the insanity of vampiric influence that muddled human minds.

And mine.

I knew I would hurt him. I'd hurt him so much, and I shouldn't care because it was my life, dammit, my future, and I had to choose what was right for me. I didn't owe anyone all of myself. I wasn't that noble, no matter what the bait for the trap.

"Cora? You okay in there?" Geoff's voice came from the direction of the living area.

"Yeah," I said. "Just flossing. I think I got some popcorn stuck in my teeth."

Why couldn't I seem to get through an hour without lying to Geoff?

I had never lied to Dorian. I couldn't.

My hand shaking slightly, I dug in my basket of toiletries and got out the birth control pack I'd gotten from the Health Center a week before. I swallowed a pill quickly—just in case.

I toweled my face dry and opened the door. Geoff had pulled off his coat and was sitting on my Gramma's couch. I hung mine up next to his.

"I used Chelsea and Christina's bathroom. I hope they'll forgive me," he said.

"What they don't know," I said. I stopped in the middle of the room, suddenly self-conscious. Conscious of what I was going to do—with Geoff and to Dorian.

"So, got a movie or something you want to put on?" Geoff asked, breaking the silence.

"We just saw a movie," I pointed out.

"There are others."

"I think you're just trying to get me on the couch," I said, sitting down next to him. My limbs felt like tubes of sand. Ghosts of sensations danced over my body, echoes of words in my mind.

To the ends of the earth.

I shivered.

"Could be, could be," Geoff said, not noticing. "Now you'll never know."

Before those phantoms could hold me back, I kissed him. Geoff kissed back, holding me against him, his hands at my waist, sliding against the skin of my back under my shirt. And Dorian was still there, filling my mind, crowding Geoff out with a sudden, keening need.

29

I pushed back without mercy, holding Geoff against me, holding onto the promise of getting back the life that had been stolen twice, first by cancer and then by the unwanted bond.

Geoff's breath was coming faster. He kissed my neck, his mouth hot and impatient, and the thrill of visceral awareness went through me. Was I ready for this? Did I want this decision? Did I even want Geoff this much, right now, or did I just want the freedom he could give me?

Freedom—and loss. Dorian would never touch me again, never kiss me, never speak to me, never look at me with those sad eyes that seemed to see into eternity—

"No." The word was a gasp, and my heart contracted so hard that it hurt. "Geoff, no, I can't do this right now. I'm sorry. It's too fast."

He sat back, releasing me suddenly, and let out a breath. "I know. It is. Something came over me, I guess. I hadn't planned—" He broke off. "I don't want to ruin this, Cora."

"We've got time," I said. I heard the echo of Dorian's words as soon as I had said them, and I bit my lip. If Geoff and I had time, then Dorian and I didn't.

And vice versa.

Why couldn't I let Dorian go? Wasn't that what I wanted—all I'd wanted?

"Sure," he said. "I've waited three years already."

"Don't even pretend you didn't date anyone else in that time," I objected, relaxing.

He grinned. "Yeah. But they weren't you, so it

doesn't count."

I gave an incredulous guffaw and socked him, and then he started tickling me, and I tickled him back until we lay in a laughing, tangled, panting heap, the tension between us dissipated into friendly companionship again.

On the outside, at least, everything was fine. And on the inside, I was shattered.

We surfed Cracked and Distractify for the next half hour, but I don't know what we saw even though I heard my laugh mingling with Geoff's, just a beat behind, and I heard my words answering him. Geoff said goodnight with a final kiss at the door. I shut it behind him and leaned against it for a long time.

Three years, he had said. And Dorian had waited, what, many hundreds?

Was it any less real, what I had with Dorian, because it was arbitrary? Was human love so much more selective that I could condemn it? It was certainly less constant, Dorian had pointed out.

I closed my eyes, and I could almost feel him with me. I had the sudden, insane impulse to call him, to tell him to come and get me and whisk me away forever and end the war that raged within me and make me happy, happy despite myself.

I took a shuddering breath and opened my eyes.

Maybe it wasn't really Dorian I distrusted so much.

Maybe it was me.

CHAPTER FOUR

When I turned off the alarm on my phone the next morning, I realized that I'd missed two calls. I hit the voicemail button before I got out of bed, rubbing at the tension in the center of my forehead—a side effect of a birth control pill in a cognate's system.

I was still a cognate. Still bound to Dorian, because I couldn't open my hand to let him go.

I'd messed up last night. I was sure of that much—but in which direction, I didn't dare to let myself think.

The first message was from Lisette, demanding to know about the date. She'd called while we were still in the movie. I rolled my eyes. It was a good thing I'd turned my ringer off.

The second was from the real estate agent who was handling Gramma's house.

"Hi, Cora. This is Beth Reid. I just wanted to let

you know that I'd really like to do an open house next week. The market seems to be picking up, and the landlord finally evicted those tenants across the street and got the yard cleaned up and looking nice, so I think just a quick push might get a contract on the house. I'm going to relist it, too, so it doesn't seem so stale. Anyhow, if you could maybe come by and just clean up a little so it looks just perfect, that'd be great. Looking to hear from you, and I hope you had a great Christmas! Bye!"

I sighed as I checked the timestamp. I hadn't been able to do the fall yard pickup that year, and the leaves from the maple tree out front were probably six inches deep.

Well, I thought to myself. *It's something else to keep me busy.*

Busy and not thinking about Dorian or about Cosimo or my date with Geoff.

I ate breakfast, packed a lunch, and called Beth back as I got into my car, telling her that I was going over right away. She thanked me and again hoped that I'd had a good Christmas, and then we hung up.

The drive to Glen Burnie was just short of an hour. I'd brought my earbuds with the mic so that I could call Lisette because I knew she would explode if she didn't have the details of my date with Geoff right away. She, of course, took full credit for the date, having brought us both out to the mall the day before, and she just about crowed with self-congratulations when I told her that we'd both had fun.

"And did you kiss?" she demanded.

"Give me a break, Lisette. It's not like it's my first kiss ever," I said.

"So you did!" she said.

"Actually, I'll have you know that even Geoff and I have kissed before," I said.

"Cora Ann Shaw," Lisette said in a scandalized tone, "how dared you not to have told me?"

"Because it isn't about you, Lisette," I said. "It's about me. And Geoff."

"But I'm your best friend. You pretty much have to tell me," she countered.

"I don't think that's anywhere in the best friend contract."

"Did you have sex?" she pushed.

"Lisette! Really. No, we didn't, and if we do, I'm not going to tell you," I said.

"Dish, dish," she urged. "So what did he do? What was it like?"

"We had dinner and watched a movie," I said. "And it was nice."

"That wasn't what I was asking." Her tone was reproachful.

"It's all I'm going to tell you, though, so you'll just have to be satisfied," I said.

"Fine then, party pooper. So when are you going out again?"

"Party pooper? Seriously, do real people even say that?" I said as I turned onto 695, heading east along the southernmost edge of Baltimore. "And I don't know. We didn't talk about it. Maybe Friday. I don't know. But I don't know if it will work out."

Those last words—I hadn't meant to say them. But once they had been said, I couldn't take them back.

"What do you mean?" Lisette demanded, her voice suddenly shrill. "You and Geoff are perfect for each other."

He was perfect for my old life. And I loved my old life. I wanted it.

Didn't I?

"I just don't know, Lisette," I said lamely.

"It's that CEO guy, isn't it?" Lisette's voice dripped with disapproval. "Does Geoff know about him?"

"Maybe that's part of it," I said. "And not that it's any of his business, but I told Geoff that I'd be going to the party of a friend from the clinic on New Year's Eve. But maybe I'm also not entirely the same person that I was before I got sick. I had everything all worked out, but now.... I don't know."

I seemed to be saying that an awful lot.

"You didn't get rejected from the University of Chicago, did you?"

"No. Actually, I just got accepted," I said.

"Then what's the problem? You're going to Chicago. He's going to Chicago—"

"He might be going to Chicago. He might also be going to UC Berkley."

"So what's the hang-up? Don't tell me the rich douche has swept you off your feet," Lisette said.

Off my feet. Out of my mind.

I tightened my grip on the steering wheel. I hated fighting with Lisette—if for no other reason than she almost always won.

"His name is Dorian. And we're not dating," I said.

"He kind of gave you a necklace worth a king's ransom, or so you said," she said. "I think that qualifies as dating."

I sighed. "I don't know. I don't know what I'm going to do."

"You've known Geoff for three and a half years," Lisette said. "You don't really know this guy at all. Don't throw Geoff over just because this Dorian guy's dazzled you."

Dazzled. If only she knew.

"God, Lisette, please don't preach at me. I don't want to hurt Geoff. And I like him—I do. I just don't know what I'm going to do right now. I feel like everything is changing under my feet."

"Nothing's changed except you," Lisette snapped. "You haven't been yourself since Christmas Eve. Look, I know you've gone through a lot, and I'm sure that knowing that you're going to be okay is a huge relief and everything, but you can't let that change who you are. You didn't let the cancer beat you. Don't let getting better mess with your head, either."

"I'm sorry," I said, deflated. The exit for I-97 loomed ahead, and I took it south to Glen Burnie. "I know I've been weird and I'm really sorry. A lot of stuff's come up recently, and I just don't know what I'm going to do about it."

"Well, whatever you do, don't forget your friends. We've been here for you for a long time," she said.

And Dorian wanted to be there for me forever....

"Yeah," I said aloud. "I know. Look, I'll talk to you

later."

"Sure. Don't forget to keep in touch," Lisette said, a touch of accusation in her tone.

"I won't," I promised. "Bye."

I hung up, and my mind went back to the circles that had already worn grooves into my brain.

What did I want? If only I could answer that question. I'd thought I wanted a way out. I'd been fighting the bond with every bit of strength that I had since I'd woken to discover what Dorian had done to me.

And now the door was open. I had a way out. And once out, I could never come back.

I wasn't sure I wanted to go.

Why not? What did I feel toward him, really? My heart went wild at the brush of his fingers, my body tuned to his every desire. He terrified me, his power over me as well as the cold political calculations that ruled his life. His ideals were almost as frightening, as was the place that they demanded that I fulfill. I had no doubt that what he felt for me, whatever name I gave it, was deep and real.

And I knew that, right now, if I had to, I would die for him.

But the only way we could have anything was through our bond. And keeping it meant something more insidious than death. It meant that I had to give up myself—if not tomorrow, then over time, as my old self was slowly altered and worn away by the force of Dorian's will, whether he meant to or not.

If breaking the bond meant that everything I felt for him was gone, then it wasn't real at all. But what if only some of it left? What if I was left with something that was very real, quite apart from whatever chemical changes tied us together?

What if I would never be the same again?

I still have time. I don't have to make the decision right now.

But if I didn't make it, I soon wouldn't be able to.

I pulled up to the small ranch house at half-past eleven. It was orange brick from the ground to the high horizontal slider windows, with white siding and black shutters above. It looked like a dozen other houses in the neighborhood—small, dated, and unremarkable. Other ranch houses had an adorable cottage vibe or at the least had a big living room picture window to let in the light. My Gramma's didn't really have anything about it that someone might find particularly attractive.

But stepping into the yard still felt like coming home. And for a moment, at least, I could put Dorian out of my mind.

I reached up to the sun visor and hit the button on the opener to the single car garage. It shuddered open reluctantly, creaking in protest. Adjusting my earbuds, I started up my peppiest playlist and got out of the car. I'd already slathered myself with sunblock, and I wore my sunglasses, a ball cap, and gloves. My cheeks had been pink with a slight sunburn after the trips to the bookstore, the Plant, and the mall yesterday. No need to risk worse.

Time to work. I smiled despite everything, feeling the strength in my body that the cancer had tried to steal away. I'd never been so happy to do a menial task.

Stray leaves on the driveway crunched under my

feet as I approached the garage. I got the big old wooden leaf rake and a box of garden bags and got started. The work was comforting, mindless and repetitive, and I was quickly able to lose myself in it.

No one stirred in the houses around me. Old Mrs. Quinlan had moved in with her daughter's family the year before last, and the rest of the neighbors that I knew were at work at that time of day. Not that I particularly wanted to see them. They always wanted to talk about Gramma, and I was out of things to say. She had died. She was gone. And I missed her. There were no words that could bring her back or pay her for the years she'd given me.

It didn't take long to clear the small yard and make a neat line of bags at the curb for pickup. During the growing season, I'd paid a neighbor's kid thirty bucks every other week to do mowing, so at least the grass looked decent under the leaves. I made a quick circuit of the house to pull weeds and prune shrubs, though that didn't really fix the fact that the bushes had mostly grown out of their spaces.

Surveying my work from the curb, I tied up the last lawn bag. It was still a small, unimpressive house with 1960s styling and 1980s siding. But it looked loved now, as it should.

I put up the lawn equipment and got the lunch I'd packed out of the car, stepping through the garage into the kitchen. I stopped just inside the door.

It still smelled the same. It was a more than a year after my Gramma had gone, nearly five months after I had packed up or sold the last of her belongings, and it still smelled like her house.

I blinked away the tears that suddenly sprang to my eyes as I unwrapped the sandwich I had packed. I sat down on the floor with my back to the door and ate it slowly.

I could almost see her standing in front of the stove with yet another boxed dinner filling the kitchen with the smell of food. It wasn't that she couldn't cook. She'd just never had much interest in it, unless it was a dessert.

"Unless it's really bad for me, why bother?" she used to say with the mischievous smile that always made her seem younger than she was.

Of course, part of the reason she hadn't cooked much was because she was so often tired. It was hard work raising a kid when you should have been retired years before. When I'd grown old enough to realize what she'd given up to keep me, I'd tried to pitch in when I could and not burden her with anything I didn't have to. She'd never resented me or shown the least regret—about me, at least, though I knew that she missed my mom and my grandfather, who'd died in an accident when I was born.

With a deep breath, I tossed the empty bag in the kitchen trash and grabbed the broom and dustpan from their places between the refrigerator and the wall. I began to systematically attack the floors, sweeping away the dust that had accumulated since I'd last come by to clean just before school started.

I was doing fine until I walked into my Gramma's bedroom and saw the green and gold striped damask wallpaper that she had chosen when the house was built. She'd told me how she'd walked into the room six months pregnant with my mother to discover the paperhanger putting in the wallpaper upside down. She'd let out a shriek of horror, and the man had fallen and broken his arm. After that, all the construction workers had regarded her with a fearful kind of respect. And despite her dismay at the man's mistake, she'd felt too guilty about the accident to make anyone fix the wallpaper, so it was upside down still.

That silly story, told so often, hit me with a sudden intensity of longing that I hadn't felt in months.

I miss you so much.

So many nights when I was sick, I'd wanted her to hold me. And now that I was well, I wished I could tell her that it had turned out all right, after all, even more than I had ever wished for her soft lap and quiet voice.

I hadn't even gotten to say goodbye.

The broom and dustpan dropped from my hands. I slid down against the wall, hugged my knees against my chest, and cried.

CHAPTER FIVE

I cried like a little kid, all snot and tears and wracking sobs. There was no one to hear.

There was no one to care.

Gramma had been dying of congestive heart failure, and she'd never told me. My last summer with her, I'd seen how she was slowing down, struggling with everyday tasks. She'd managed to hide her illness so well that I'd felt only concern, not alarm, during my visits every Sunday to drive her to St. Paul's and then run her errands and help out around the house. She covered her struggles with the excuse that she was just a little "tired" from some activity or other that she had done earlier in the week. Each time, it was a new excuse, and each time, I believed her.

She'd been so determined to be there for me when I was little, that I would have a normal experience growing up despite how much older she was than my friends' parents, that she hadn't even told me when she needed me to be there for her.

And then one day, when her friend dropped by for her weekly visit, she was dead. My Gramma died alone, with no one to hold her hand. No one to even know for two long days. Mrs. Turow had called me with the news, and only then had I learned that she'd been sick at all.

I would've wanted to be there, damn school and my grades and everything else. Gramma was more important than all those things. But she'd given up even my being with her in her last weeks for fear of being a burden on me, afraid she'd be keeping me from the life she thought I would have had if my mother had lived.

I wished I could tell her now that it was going to turn out okay. Because it had to, didn't it? I wasn't sick anymore. I was still the girl that she'd known, still going to have the happy life that she'd wanted for me. I was still going to make her proud....

And how could Dorian fit into any of that? He didn't have a place in that life, the life my Gramma had given up so much for. I could have been free of him forever last night, but I couldn't let go. And now I was afraid that after everything she'd done to give me a good life, I was going to throw it all away because I was weak and stupid and drugged with sex and addicted to a vampire's presence.

Gradually, my sobs turned to sniffles. I paused the music app, abruptly silencing Jason Mraz's voice, and stumbled into the bathroom to discover that the toilet paper roll was empty. Sniffing hard, I got another from under the sink mechanically, changed it out, and pulled off a good length to blow my nose. I flushed it, noticing the slight ring of lime around the toilet as I did so.

I closed my eyes. I'd take care of that, too. I'd take care of everything.

I picked up the broom and finished the floors in the bedroom and bath. Then I washed down all the tile counters in the bathrooms and kitchen and wiped out the sinks. All the windowsills got a pass with a wet sponge, and every corner of the house was cleared of spider webs with a towel knotted over the end of the broom.

Crying or not, there was no one to do it but me.

Finally, I set to work on the toilets, which had calcified rings at the waterline from neglect and disuse, scrubbing with single-minded determination.

"You should try vinegar."

I jumped so hard at the voice that I launched myself backwards into the bathtub, knocking my spine and elbow into it as the toilet brush went flying.

Dorian stood leaning in the doorway of the bathroom and looking down at me in a three-piece suit, as handsome as the devil himself. His jet black hair was impeccably arranged, his blue eyes piercing under the dark wings of his brows. I had no idea how I hadn't noticed his approach, because the force of his presence was almost too much in the tiny room.

My blood sang in my ears, terror and relief and joy all mixed up until I didn't know where one feeling stopped and the next began.

And all I could do was rub my throbbing elbow and stare at the beautiful not-man who had come for me. He was still mine. Or I was still his. It was hard in that moment to believe that it mattered much which it was.

Finally, I found my voice. "What are you doing here? You scared me to death."

But my heart was hammering for reasons other than surprise. Oh, God, I was so glad to see him, so glad even in the midst of my fear. I didn't know that I could be so glad to see anyone.

I had almost lost him the night before—had almost given him up, thrown him away. Now, that seemed like madness.

Please don't leave me, I thought. *Don't let me leave—*

I slammed a door down on those thoughts.

"I didn't realize that I was sneaking." He stepped inside, reached across me, and retrieved the toilet scrubber, offering it to me handle-first.

I took it.

"How do you know about cleaning toilets, anyway?" I asked, covering my reaction behind a curtain of hair as I went back to attacking the toilet ring.

"I've owned a few disused properties in my time," he said. "If you fill it with vinegar and let it sit for a day or two, it will eat away the lime without hurting the porcelain."

"That really works?"

"Like a charm," he said.

Like a charm. Funny, those words, so easy and casual. They weren't the kind of thing I could imagine him saying even a few days ago.

But I said, "Do you have any vinegar?" It was always a strange sensation when Dorian revealed knowledge about some everyday matter. Somehow, he seemed above the world, apart from it. I wasn't sure I liked it when he showed himself to be as real as anything else.

As anyone else.

"Not on me at the moment," he said.

"Neither do I." I paused, sitting back on my heels and looking at him. "You never answered my question. What are you doing here?"

"I told you that I can tell if you are feeling an intense emotion," he said.

I remembered my uncontrolled crying jag. Yeah. That would certainly qualify. No one to care, I'd thought. But I'd been wrong. Dorian had cared.

He would always care.

"I guess I was pretty upset," I said.

"And now?" he prompted.

"Better now," I said. I dropped my eyes and resumed scrubbing.

He touched my shoulder, giving it the smallest squeeze, and I leaned into the contact. It felt better than it should, dangerously reassuring.

And when he spoke again, Dorian's voice colored with echoes of an unreadable emotion. "You were so deeply disturbed, Cora. I had to call off the rest of the team when I realized you weren't in actual physical danger."

"The rest of the team?" I echoed. "You mean like when you came to get me when I was being chased?" He'd used the GPS software he'd installed on my phone and car to find me then—as I assumed he had this time, too.

"Given the intensity of your response, I was close to panic," he said.

Those words startled me enough that I looked into his impassive, inscrutable face. He was as impossibly collected as ever, and yet the speed at which he had arrived gave weight to his words, and I didn't doubt them.

Dorian Thorne, the ageless, powerful vampire. In a panic, for me.

"I'm twenty-one, my family's all dead, and I just recently nearly died, too, only to be saved by a vampire who seems to want my soul in exchange," I said aloud. "I think I have reason to be disturbed, as you call it."

"I'm sorry, Cora. I don't want to cause you pain."

His words were quiet, and I caught a fleeting glimpse of that old, haunted expression pass over his face. And it hurt me.

I sighed. "I know. I'm just afraid that you'll decide that you don't want to cause me pain so much that you make it so I don't feel it anymore."

He plucked the scrubber and cleaner from my hands, setting them on the counter, and pulled me to my feet. His touch set my whole body to humming, and I realized how much I had wanted it, how much I had missed it.

I couldn't make myself let go of his hand. The

night before, I had almost—I couldn't even finish the thought.

Was I crazy then? Am I crazy now?

"I won't do that, Cora." His free hand stroked my cheek tenderly, sending a bittersweet yearning through me, and I almost started crying again.

"You wouldn't do it on purpose," I said. "For now."

"Ever," he insisted.

"What if I ask you to?" I whispered. "I don't want to be changed. I don't. But I don't want to hurt, either, and I can be weak and stupid, and in a rash moment—"

He kissed me, gently, stopping my words. My entire body ached at his touch, but I only stood there, frozen, like a rabbit that had seen a fox. "I won't, Cora, I promise. Even if you ask."

He pulled my head against his chest, and I leaned into him, his strength supporting me. "Not even for your damned Adelphoi?"

His arms tightened fractionally. "I do only what I must."

I whispered, "Must is such a funny word. If you do change me, the only thing you risk is your principles. I could lose myself."

I could feel his words in his chest as he answered. "Sometimes principles are the most important thing. Sometimes, they are the only thing."

"The only thing?" I echoed, looking up at him.

His smile was disarming. "Between me and madness."

I felt a slight chill because I knew, despite the lightness of his words, that he was deadly serious.

"And you're not mad," I said, both a statement and a question.

"Not yet," he agreed. "And I never will be, as long as I have you."

How long would that be? I wondered. I wanted to demand why he hadn't told me that the bond could be broken. But Dorian had been hiding it from me on purpose, and whatever reason he had, he might consider it one of those troubling cases of the greater good that I not find out or that I forget that I ever knew.

I took a shuddering breath. With all my willpower, I disengaged myself from him and stashed the toilet scrubber and cleaner in the vanity, then wiped down the counter a final time. The ring of lime around the toilet was slightly lighter now, but it was still there.

"Thanks for worrying about me," I said, grabbing the kitchen trash can from the back of the room. I was surprised to realize how much I meant it. "It's just a bit weird to have someone sense my feelings psychically and fly to my side. I'm not actually sure how much I like that." I'd never grieve alone with him, not really, and sometimes, grief didn't want to be shared. "But I'm glad you care."

"Of course I care." He stepped out of the way so that I could leave the bathroom.

"Would you, though?" I asked, going to the kitchen. "Without the bond, I mean."

"That's like asking a human if they would love if they weren't in love," he objected. "It makes no sense."

I put the trash can in its place under the kitchen

sink and turned to face him. "This isn't the first time you've said that word. Love. What does it mean to you? What can it mean?"

He stepped up to me so that I was trapped between his body and the sink, pulling me to him. "What does it mean to anyone, Cora? You tell me. What is this love that you want to talk so much about?"

I stood there, in my Gramma's kitchen, my body against this man, this falling angel or rising demon who had claimed me as his own. And I thought of my Gramma, Sally Lowden, who had given so much of herself.

"Love is caring," I said. "Self-sacrifice. Kindness. Patience. Connection. Compassion and sympathy."

"And romantic love?" he pressed. "What more is it?"

"I don't know," I said.

"You do," he countered. "You must, or you wouldn't be asking me about it."

I closed my eyes. His arm around me was sending small flutters through my body that I did not want to examine too closely. That I couldn't examine, right now.

"Desire is a part of it, but it has to be more than that," I breathed. "A sense of being one with another person, like you found the missing part of yourself. Wanting them and wanting their happiness like it's your own. And a connection again—"

"A bond," he said.

My eyes flew open.

He said, "In humans, you could choose to classify love as a mere physiological reaction, a cascade of hormones, serotonin and oxytocin and a touch of adrenaline for desire. At times, such things strike, as the cliché goes, from across a crowded room."

"But that's just the desire part," I protested.

"It's the start of love," he said. His arms tightened around me. "When I first saw you, I almost lost control of myself for the first time in several centuries. Don't tell me that you didn't feel it, too."

"But you influence all humans," I said. "There was nothing special about me."

"I can influence all humans to varying degrees, but not often like *that*."

I rocked softly in his arms, remembering the power he held over me even then, the awareness and wanting that he had sent through my body to befuddle my senses, clouding my mind like nothing I had ever felt before.

"I'm not sure what I felt. You were very overpowering. I don't know really what it was. I'm still not sure."

"I think you are just afraid of giving it a name," he said. "Even then, I wanted you to be the one so badly that it hurt."

"And when you bit me—" I broke off, unable even now to talk about the hideous, glorious, ecstatic madness of that night.

"The potential was made fully real," he said.

"The bond," I said. "But it's so arbitrary. It might have been anyone!"

He shook his head. "Any *one* in ten thousand. How many boys did you expect to date before finding one you could love and settling down? Three? Five? Twenty? Not ten thousand, I'm sure."

I opened my mouth, then closed it, unable to counter his point. Everything rose up together to overwhelm me, my battered emotions, the strangeness of the past week, the insanity of my position—and most of all him, holding me, stroking me.

Maybe even loving me, like I was afraid that I wanted him to.

"Just kiss me," I whispered. "Kiss me now."

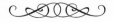

Chapter Six

And he did, taking my mouth with his own. I looped my arms over his neck, clinging to him, needing him, wanting him like I had never wanted anything in my life as he caressed me with his hands and tongue until my body was consumed in his rhythm and his strength.

Finally, slowly, I pulled away. He rested his forehead against mine. For a long moment he just held me, and we breathed.

He broke the silence. "You're wearing the necklace."

"Yeah." My hand strayed to my neck, where the lump of the pendant lay under my shirt. I had put it on the night before as soon as Geoff had left, and I hadn't taken it off since.

I didn't know what I meant by it. I didn't know

anything, right now.

I took a shuddering breath and changed the subject. "I'm done here. I should probably head back to my apartment."

Home. I should have said home. But I wasn't really sure where my home was. This house had been my home for so many years, but now it was empty, barren, ready for someone else to make it theirs. My apartment was where I lived with Lisette, but nothing about it was truly mine. And Dorian's house...he wanted it to be mine, too, I knew. But as huge as it was, I wasn't sure there was room for me there.

"I'll drive you," Dorian said.

"What about my car?" I said.

"I'll have someone drop it off at your apartment," he said. "We'll leave the keys under the doormat here."

I hesitated for a moment. "Okay, I guess," I said. It seemed a waste for him to come out here for nothing, I rationalized.

But I knew that really, I just didn't want him to go. Not when I'd come so close to losing him.

I looked around my Gramma's empty kitchen one last time. If nothing she had wanted for me came true, would everything she'd given me still matter?

Shaking off that thought, I bundled up, and we went out through the garage. I stopped at the sight of the car behind mine in the driveway.

"Seriously?" I asked. "How many cars do you have?"

He chuckled, coming up behind me. "Is it wrong to say that I'm not really sure? That's my newest Aston

Martin."

"I don't really know much about cars," I admitted.

"Keys?" He held out his hand.

"Let me get the garage door first," I said. I ducked into my car and hit the door opener clipped to the visor, then locked the car, pulled the key off my key ring, and handed it to Dorian. I watched as he slid it under the front doormat.

"Ready to go?" he asked.

"Sure."

He opened the door for me, and I climbed into his car.

"Aston Martin," I repeated as he swung in and shut the door. "I'm Bond. James Bond." Which pretty much exhausted everything I knew about the manufacturer.

"I'm afraid this car is lacking in the high-tech weaponry department," he said dryly.

"Ha! So you aren't entirely oblivious of pop culture," I said.

He backed out of the driveway and turned down the street. "Not entirely, no." He paused. "So, the house...."

"It was my Gramma's. Mine, too. Where I grew up," I said, glad to be talking of something less dangerous than love. "She died last year, right after Thanksgiving, and it took me months to go through probate and to get it ready to sell. It finally went on the market in October, but no offers yet. There were some renters across the street who'd really junked up the place, but they got kicked out, so my real estate agent is hoping that we'll get a bite if we do a showcase this weekend. I was cleaning it up for that."

"And she was the last of your family." His voice was perfectly neutral. Of course he knew that—he'd said that he'd known from my medical records that I had no next-of-kin.

I recited the canned explanation that I'd given so many times before. "My parents were both only children. They died in a car crash with my grandfather. It had been raining, and there was a low spot on the road with too much standing water on a curve. It was dark, too dark to see the water, and our car hydroplaned and crossed the center line into a semi. My mom survived just long enough to give birth to me, four weeks premature, and Gramma raised me alone."

"Do you not have any extended relatives? Distant cousins, great-aunts and uncles?"

I shrugged. "My grandfather had two brothers. I met their families a couple of times, but that was all. My dad was estranged from his family. I tried to track them down once, when I was a teenager, but they didn't want to have anything to do with me."

"So it truly was just you and your grandmother."

I couldn't quite tell what he thought of that—whether it meant anything to him at all since he had forgotten his own family in the mists of time.

I said, "It was enough. It really was. She was sixty-three when I was born. Eighty-two when she died. I was so sure she would live to be ninety, or maybe a hundred. I don't know why. She just always seemed so full of life. I wanted her to see me married. See my kids. I wanted her to hold them, to know that everything had worked out in the end."

Dorian looked over at me, compassion in his fathomless eyes. "I couldn't imagine that she was disappointed."

"I know she wasn't." How could I explain how my heart ached for what she hadn't seen? "I just wanted her to see me have all the things my mom never got, all the things she wanted me to have. So she'd know it really was okay." I took a shaky breath.

In the long silence, Dorian reached out and captured my hand in his, squeezing it, the contact as comforting as it was arousing. I blinked away the sudden tears, grateful that he left the easy platitudes unsaid.

Wishing I knew what I should do.

When he finally spoke, his words took me by surprise. "You don't have to sell the house if you don't want to."

My breath froze in my lungs. "What?"

His eyes did not leave the road. "My resources are at your disposal. Whatever money you need, I can supply. You don't need to sell your grandmother's house to pay for anything."

I considered it for a wild moment, taking down the For Sale sign and just locking the door and all my memories inside, hoarding them inside my heart....

Then I sighed. "No. I'm not going to live in the house again, and Gramma wouldn't want it to sit there empty. It's time for it to be a home to someone else's family."

"Fair enough," he said, his voice gentler than his light words. He freed his hand to shift gears, and I tried not to feel the loss of his touch.

"What about you?" I asked, studying his aristocratic profile. "Surely you remember something from your childhood. Anything at all."

The sadness was back again, and an expression of such distance that he seemed to be a world away. "I've already told you that I don't have any memories, only their echoes."

Gramma had always told me how excited my mother was to have me, how much she'd loved me, how proud my father had been. It had never been fully real, just words to go along with the happy wedding pictures in the living room.

But I'd had Gramma, twenty years of memories with her, and I had never lacked for love. And I'd never forget it, no matter how many years went by.

Dorian looked over at me. "Come home with me, Cora. You shouldn't be alone right now."

I bit my lip. Always, I had yielded to him, either because of the undeniable reasonableness of his arguments or because he forced me to. Even when he'd taken me home after the Lesser Introduction, it had been at his prompting. I needed to have my way just this once, just to know that I could.

"No," I said. "I want to go to my apartment."

He appeared to think about it for a moment, then nodded. "All right."

And that was it.

It was, I decided, a bit of a letdown.

"I don't really know that much about you, you know," I said aloud. "I mean, considering that you're supposed to be my one-and-only."

He lifted a shoulder negligently. "We are learning about one another together. There's no rush."

But there was, and I couldn't tell him what it was, couldn't confess that for me absolutely everything was at stake....

The headlights flicked on automatically in the gathering gloom, and he pulled his sunglasses off. Self-consciously, I did the same.

"It's a bit easier for you, I think. There just isn't that much to learn about, with me," I said.

"You sell yourself short," he said.

I snorted. "I'm twenty-one. You're, what, fifty times that? One hundred times?"

"More," he said evenly. "How much more, I don't know."

I drew a breath. Despite everything, the answer still threw me a little off guard. "How about we take turns, then?" I kept my voice light. "You ask me a question, and then I ask you one."

He looked amused. "That works for me."

I pushed my hair back behind my ear. "I'll go first. What exactly do you do for a living? You're obviously well off, and I met you at your office, but you were here on a Wednesday when I woke up, so you don't exactly seem to be working eighty hours a week."

"I work in investments and real estate, mostly, and of course the medical research, but the last is more an expenditure than income, at least for now." He glanced at me. "Before you came, I was working...perhaps too much."

There seemed to be a wealth of things unsaid in that last sentence, but his expression was inscrutable.

"But not right now," I pressed, seeking confirmation.

"Things change. You've changed them." Before I could follow that up, he changed the subject abruptly. "My turn. Where do you want to go to grad school, and why not the University of Maryland?"

"Chicago," I blurted. He'd remembered about that, and I was grateful for that even as I was afraid of my own gratitude. "I've been accepted. It's got a better program, one of the best in the country, and definitely the one with the most interesting schools of economic philosophy."

"You can get a job at any one of my companies without it," he said, casting a sideways glance at me.

I shook my head. "I'm not going to work for my boyfriend's company."

Boyfriend. I had said the word. Why had I said that word?

"I'm not your *boyfriend*, and you could consider them all to be your companies, as well," he said.

"Vampires don't do prenups?" I joked to distract myself.

"They are not necessary."

All traces of amusement fled. No, when an agnate had such utter control over a cognate, a prenup would be redundant.

"The bond never falters, Cora," he said as if he could read my mind. "As long as it persists, it never changes and it never fails."

"So a cognate would never betray an agnate," I said, thinking of what I had almost done with Geoff the night before.

"That is not what I said." His eyes went through me.

He knows, I thought. *He must know.*

Then he returned his gaze to the road, and I chided myself for letting my guilt send me spiraling into paranoia.

"It's your turn," he said after a long silence. "The question about prenups hardly counts, I think."

"Of course," I said.

I had too many questions, most of which I didn't even know how to ask. I chose one that, as trivial as it was, had been niggling at my mind for a while. Every time I pictured Dorian alone, he was brooding over his laptop in the cavern of his office or in the great stone mausoleum of his house. No one could really live like that. Could they?

I remembered something that Cosimo had said about Dorian not being able to feel anymore without me. Maybe that's all there had been to him then, that maybe he had...worn thin, over the years. Grown hollow.

Aloud, I asked, "So what do you do for fun?" That sounded stupid, so I tried again. "What are your hobbies? Your entertainment?" What I really meant was, *What were you, before I was here?*

"Fun." He said the word as if he were trying it out, his expression remote. "I haven't done much for fun in...a while."

In years, my mind substituted for those two words. Perhaps a lifetime.

"I suppose I fell out of the habit," he continued. "In the past, though, I frequented every kind of diversion, high and low. Movies, the theater, the opera, concerts. Aviation, boating, riding—racing practically anything in my more reckless days. I still collect cars, out of habit, I suppose. Music. Drinking and gambling, even, once. At some point, I've been through every recreational activity that humans have invented and then some."

I hugged myself, thinking of the wilder vampire gatherings that I had seen. But I could refer to only some of it, or else I'd have to confess to Cosimo's field trip. "Drugs? Like those agnates who got in the fight at your party?"

Dorian's reply was steady. "I chased the rush, too, once, when I thought I had nothing left to live for. But my last descent predated the poisons that humans and agnates alike now pursue. Still, any human drug is positively benign for an agnate compared to the risks of, say, early aviation."

"I can't imagine you like that," I said.

"When every day feels like you've already been through it a thousand times, and even the air tastes like you've breathed it before, and still the days keep on marching, one after the next, forever, without end.... It's just existence. Tedious. Interminable. Some sink into that, lose all ability to feel and, eventually, even think. Most rebel, trying anything in the world to feel alive again...." His face briefly creased in a frown, a fleeting expression passing across his face that contained the echoes of a pain I couldn't fully understand.

A pain I'd almost added to.

Watching the string of taillights down the tree-lined monotony of the Baltimore-Washington Parkway, I tried to imagine my Dorian, so calm and collected, flinging aside his enormous self-control and chasing the rush with the same intensity that he devoted to everything else. It was an unsettling thought.

"Do you feel like that now at all?" I asked. "Like the air is old and all the rest, I mean."

He looked at me. "No. Not with you."

The words were simple, almost blunt, but I was suddenly excruciatingly aware of him sitting so close to me and the power that his inhuman beauty held over me. My breath tangling in my lungs, I clenched my hands in my lap to keep from reaching out to touch him.

He turned back to the road and continued. "I found a cause, a reason for living, in my research. But you remind me now of the hobbies I cultivated once—not as a rusher but merely as an amateur in the oldest sense. They fell away, so gradually that I didn't even realize how far I'd gone, but I suppose that's always the way of it, our eroding of the mind. It starts as indifference and ends in senility, a living death even as our bodies continue on."

I remembered the agnate at the buffet during my introduction, mumbling to herself as she scooped food messily onto her plate. My mind shuddered away from that thought.

The buildings outside the car window were familiar—the red brick of the College Park campus. We were almost at my apartment. Time had passed quickly, too quickly. Dorian pulled into the mostly empty parking lot, like he had the other night.

"Inviting yourself up again?" I asked.

"Only if you want me to," he said. He pulled into a space and put the car in park. Unbuckling, he turned to face me.

The impossibility of my situation came over me again. How could I let him have all of me?

How could I possibly refuse?

"What's your end game, Dorian?" I asked abruptly.

For once, I seemed to surprise him, and his eyebrows rose. "What do you mean?"

"What's your goal? What's your plan for me?" I asked.

"I don't make plans for you, Cora." Dorian touched me lightly, just his fingertips brushing against the back of my hand, and my entire body thrilled with it.

I pulled away. "No, you just have huge parties where I'm the main attraction. You're weaving your webs, you monsters with a conscience versus those without, and I'm a symbol for you in it. I know you can't afford to have this go wrong. So what will you sacrifice to make sure that it doesn't?"

"It won't," he said simply.

I scrubbed my face in frustration. "How could you know that? I could be a terrible person. You could have bonded with anyone, and you'd gamble everything on that person being just right for you?"

His hooded eyes never left my face. "I bonded with you, Cora, not just anyone. And I know what you are, perhaps better than you know it yourself. What we have—it will work. It must work."

"But what if I don't want it to? I want to finish my degree, go to grad school, get a job."

Dorian shook his head. "I won't stop you from doing any of that."

"Even if I want to go to Chicago? You'll change me," I said hopelessly. "You do change me."

"I've given my word that I won't...mess with your head, as you call it, not unless the alternative is unthinkable."

How could I make him understand? If I left him—when I left him—he needed to understand why I had to do it. Maybe then I would hurt him less, or at least the wounds would heal a little faster.

I said, "You mess with my head all the time. You might not be deliberately rearranging my thoughts, but you still do it. Every time I'm near you, I can feel your will and your desires, wrapping around me. I'm helpless in them."

"I may be the stronger, Cora, but I feel yours, too," he said softly.

"It's not the same."

"Perhaps not." He reached out, placing his palm flat above my left breast. "But I can feel how your heart is torn. I can feel you yearning for me but afraid. I can feel what you desire most, Cora, and I want to do everything in my power to fulfill those dreams."

My heart thudded against his hand. "But you'll still

change me. You can't help it."

He look old suddenly, as old as mountains. "All meaningful relationships are transformative."

"More than any human relationship," I insisted.

He shook his head. "And that I can't help. But just because it is a change doesn't mean that it's bad."

I had to make him understand, somehow, why I couldn't live with that. "I want a normal life, Dorian. You can't give me that."

"Do you, Cora?" he asked softly. "Do you really?" His gaze grew intense, and I couldn't answer him.

Because I didn't know.

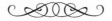

CHAPTER SEVEN

Dorian's hand slid up to cradle my cheek. Despite everything, or maybe because of it, I turned my face into it, kissing his palm. It smelled of him, the scent that had covered my body a few days before. I thought of all he had already done to me—with me. It was overwhelming, even the memory of it almost too much to bear.

And I wanted more. More of his touch but also his presence. His smiles. His solemnity and the ineffable sadness that came of regrets I didn't understand. I wanted to lay those haunting memories to rest.

I wanted his body, his kisses, his sex. And as foolish as it was, I wanted his love.

With a low sound, he pulled me toward him, meeting me across the high console that separated the seats. His mouth was impatient, hungry against mine. The dull heat in my abdomen roared to sudden fire, my groin aching with every touch of his lips and stroke of his tongue.

"Cora—" he said roughly as he broke off, a warning in his voice.

"I want it, too," I assured him.

But he shook his head. "You don't understand. It's been almost two weeks, Cora."

Two weeks? My mind went back. *Oh.* Two weeks since I had first given him my blood.

"I thought you could go for months," I said faintly, my heart accelerating.

His chuckle was ragged as he caressed the line of my jaw. "It is one thing to avoid all temptation and quite another to indulge some desires and ignore others."

I could feel his need now. It washed through me, calling up an answer from my own body, one I couldn't refuse. I could feel my breath come faster, my blood rushing through my veins, and I knew I would give him what he asked. I must. I wanted nothing else.

"Would it be like the first time?" I asked quietly. "Will I be unconscious for days?"

"No, of course not." His frown was a flat rejection. "Conversion only happens once."

I swallowed, closing my eyes, feeling the expectation twisting tighter and tighter inside me. I was going to do this thing again, knowing what was coming. I remembered the insanity of that first night, the madness and the pain and the ecstasy, the glory and terror all flowing together until I didn't know where one stopped and another began.

It really was going to happen. Again. Tonight.

"Then show me," I said, opening my eyes and meeting his gaze. My vampire. There was nothing human about him now. And somehow, it made me want him more.

Desire flared deep in his eyes.

"Your arm," he said, and he held out his hand.

I unbuckled then and turned in my seat, putting my hand in his. My insides shivered a little at the contact, my skin flushing. He pushed my sleeve up my arm, and I was reminded of our first encounter, when he had drawn my blood.

"You're willing?" he asked, looking at me with those haunted eyes.

"Yes," I breathed. "You know I am."

He lifted my wrist to his mouth. I didn't realize how tense I was until I felt the first brush against my skin, and a sizzle of reaction jolted through my body.

It was a kiss—only a kiss, a gentle caress of his lips against my skin. I took a shuddering breath. Holding my gaze, he moved up, toward my elbow, deepening his kisses until I shivered with need, heat from my center running in prickling waves across my skin.

The pressure increased, and I felt his tongue and teeth working across my arm. My breath came raggedly. And then, just above my wrist, the sudden, sharp pain as he cut into my skin.

I gasped as the heat roared up, tangling with the pain, consuming and transforming it as it surged up into my brain. His mouth set a rhythm against my arm, sealing the wound, sucking against it, and my body was seized with it, throbbing in time, need mounting higher and higher.

And his eyes never let me go. I could feel him inside my mind, could feel his need washing into mine as he drank from my veins. Finally, he broke the kiss and lowered my arm. I blinked, breaking away from his eyes, still reeling with unfulfilled desire, as he turned my wrist toward me.

My skin was whole already, only bright silvery lines showing where he had taken from me with a few faint blood-streaks on the unbroken skin.

"We're made for each other now, Cora," he said, and then he pulled me across the console into his embrace.

I could still taste the faint, metallic tang of my blood in his mouth. The need was battering me now, driving me to crazy heights. He pushed back his seat as he pulled me into his lap.

His hands were under my shirt, under my bra, moving hard across my body. I kissed him hard, wanting him, one hand fumbling at the button on my jeans as the other tangled in his hair. I got it free, unzipped my jeans, and kicked off my shoes as he pushed them over my hips, catching my panties and hauling them off, too. I grabbed the pants leg as it slid over my foot and pulled the jeans off as he loosened his belt and fly.

He leaned the seat back as he pulled me down to his mouth again. My bare legs hung over the console, my rear in his lap. I could feel his erection against my hip, separated only by the thin layer of his underwear.

He kissed me, hard, took my mouth and then bent to move to my neck. I pulled his suit jacket and waistcoat open, yanking at his shirt buttons, needing his skin against my hands. One of his palms found my breast, and I let go of his shirt and grabbed his head, pulling his mouth up to meet mine again, kissing him with an urgency that I'd never felt before. With his other hand, he pulled my knee across his lap so that I straddled him, my damp thighs opening.

His hand slid up to my entrance, teasing my clitoris with strokes of his fingers before dipping inside me to stroke the nub there while I rocked and shook against his body, my fingers digging into to his shoulders. He pushed me right up to the edge of a climax, but I felt him holding me back, and I made a sobbing noise of frustration as I reached, reached—

"Want it?" His voice was harsh in my ear.

"Now," I demanded. "Do it now."

He slid his fingers out of me and reached between us, freeing his erection. He grasped my hips and guided me over it, until the head pressed against me. Then he pulled me down hard, and I cried out as he hit the swollen sensitive place inside of me, pushing me right up to the edge. I tried to hold still, panting, but his hips were moving under me, his hands on my hips demanding that I rise and fall with him. I did, every thrust coming up against that spot and then the other, deeper one, sending hot pleasure around into my clitoris and deep into the center of my body.

He stole my gasps with his mouth, kissing them

away. One of his hands slid from my hip, across my buttocks, to press against the space between my entrance and my anus, finishing the circle of pleasure. I teetered on the brink for a long moment, moving with him in that maddening rhythm, my skin so hot I thought I would be set on fire.

"Cora." He ground out my name against my lips and shuddered underneath me, and I shattered.

The pleasure, as sharp as pain, flared up in my center and tore through my body, taking everything with it, sense, sight, and sanity. He was still pushing me onward, into the climax, and I plunged into it madly, embracing the immolation of self in the surging need.

Coming to myself again, I sank bonelessly against his bare chest.

"Oh wow. Just wow." I realized that was my own voice, and I stopped.

Dorian was stroking my hair, and I turned my head to catch him looking down at me.

"That wasn't planned," he said.

"I should hope not," I retorted. "Anyone could have walked by." The aftermath of my climax still washed through me, my skin still tender and flushed. I was almost appalled at how much I had wanted that, how much I had enjoyed it. All of it, including his teeth piercing my skin, his mouth moving against it to drink my blood.

God, he really had turned my brain inside out, hadn't he?

I pulled away, wincing as I swung my stiff leg over his thighs. There was no elegant way to slither back across the console, but I tried to retain some semblance of dignity. My bare rear hit the warm leather seat, and I reached quickly for my pants and dragged them on.

"Cora," he said, my name something between a question and an apology.

Pausing in the fumbling with my fly, I closed my eyes for a moment. "I need to go upstairs for a minute. Then—I want you to take me to your home."

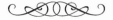

CHAPTER EIGHT

There was a long silence as I finished straightening my clothes. I didn't look at Dorian, but I could hear him doing the same.

"All right," Dorian said finally. I heard a hint of some emotion in his voice, fiercely repressed. Was it gladness? His face was completely closed, as if he didn't dare to show anything.

Was it me that he didn't trust? Or was it himself?

Dorian reached into the back to hand me my jacket. He still wore his sports coat. "Shall I come up?"

"Sure," I said. I hoped it sounded casual. In truth, I wanted him close to me so badly that it hurt.

I pulled my coat on as he stepped out of the car. He was at my door by the time I had it on, opening it and offering his hand. I took it self-consciously and stood. He shut the door behind me, and I walked silently toward my apartment block under the weight of his arm. I felt my need for him like an ache, a pain. I was far from satisfied.

I was afraid that I never would be.

"What made you change your mind?" he asked. The words were light, too light. My answer mattered too much to him.

"I don't know," I said. I frowned at him. "I really hope that the answer isn't you."

"You can't keep second-guessing every impulse, Cora," he said.

"How can't I?" I asked. "How can I ever know why I want anything, ever again?"

"Human couples grow more alike over time," Dorian said. "If your taste in music changes because your boyfriend keeps putting on a radio station different from what you normally are used to, is that a malevolent influence? If you come to enjoy a new genre of movie or a new kind of food, or if some of your preferences for clothing begin to align more with his over time, is that evidence that you've been corrupted?"

Reaching the door, I scanned my ID, and he opened it so I could pass through first.

"I suppose not," I admitted. I hit the button to call the elevator. The doors opened. I stepped inside, Dorian following.

"If you want to be with someone, perhaps it is simply because you want them," he said.

I turned to look at him, so handsome that it was

almost painful.

"I do," I heard myself say, my voice suddenly rough. "I want you."

He closed the space between us so quickly that I didn't even have time to take a breath. He pressed me against the wall of the elevator, his arms around me, under my clothes, his mouth over mine. I clung to him and kissed him back, hard.

The door chimed and opened far too soon. He stepped backward through it, pulling me with him, taking my keys from my unresisting grasp with his other hand. In moments, my door was unlocked and we were through. He closed the door with his foot as he pulled off my coat and dragged my shirt over my head. My hurried fingers fumbled with the buttons of his shirt. One caught, and I yanked, and it came free with a tearing sound.

"Sorry," I said, my hands freezing.

He just chuckled and grabbed the open edges of the shirt, and with a single motion, he tore the remaining buttons free. I heard them clatter as they bounced off the walls and floor.

"I don't know how I'll explain that one to Lisette," I said breathlessly.

"Don't, then," he said, stripping off his shirt, waistcoat, and jacket in one go. Catching my hair, he tilted my head back so that my mouth turned up to meet his.

And he tasted so good, like everything I'd ever wanted in my life.

Dorian twisted my bra free with his other hand, tugging it down over my arms, then he took my hips in his hands and worked his mouth impatiently down across my neck and collarbone.

His kisses were rough, and I craved every one of them. The bite on my wrist had aroused me to an edge of pain that I suddenly needed again, a need that he seemed to understand without my asking. My breath turned ragged, my hands holding his shoulders so hard that I felt his flesh under my fingernails.

His breath against my nipple made it harden, sending a ripple of sensation down into my clitoris, and he enveloped it in his mouth. There was nothing tender about it. He took it sharply in his teeth, his tongue rasping across the tip, and I cried out, wanting the edge of the pain in the heat of pleasure. He pulled his head back, his teeth scraping lightly along my nipple, and I gasped, my fingernails digging into his shoulders. Then it was free, damp and tingling in the chilly air.

Never had I imagined this—never would I have thought I could have wanted it so badly.

He moved to the other breast, his deep kisses turning to nips that left me shaking, arching my hips to meet a resistance that wasn't there. His mouth slid across my belly as he knelt at my feet, his hands working at my fly, and he shoved my jeans over my hips and down. Then his tongue was there, at the juncture of my thighs, working rhythmically against my clitoris as his hands slid back to cup my butt and pull me more firmly against his mouth.

I rocked in his grasp, panting, as his tongue pressed deeper, sliding between my folds. My hands balled into fists around his hair. His grip on me only tightened, pulling my buttocks apart. I knew he could taste me and what he'd spilled into me, and I didn't know whether I was more aroused or mortified.

"Dorian," I managed, not sure what I wanted to say.

He broke off, stood again, and kissed my mouth, and I could taste it, too—myself, him, mingled together in his demanding mouth.

Then he scooped me into his arms and carried me the three short strides to the sofa, where he set me down with my hips hanging over the wide arm and pulled my pants the rest of the way off, taking my shoes and socks with them. His followed. I started to wriggle up on the couch, but he grabbed my knee.

"No," he said, pulling me back. "I want you here."

He hooked one of my legs over his shoulder, sliding his hand down the inside of my thigh until it rested on my entrance, the outer folds pulled open by how he held me. He rolled my clitoris between his fingers, teasing it until my entire body felt suffused. And then he slid two fingers into me, side by side, stretching me as he found that place in front where he pressed, rhythmically, again and again as his thumb stroked above. A finger of his other hand dipped briefly into me, then pulled down, hard, so that he was at both ends of my entrance, relentless, overwhelming.

I came, clenching around his hand, the heat shooting through my body as I cried out. His lower hand slipped lower still, pushing hard against the space just behind my entrance, and then it was there, at my anus, pressing just inside as I shattered around him. It shook me again, in a way I had never felt, driving me deeper into the throes of my orgasm.

Then it was over, and his upper hand slid out of me, but the lower one was still there, the tip just inside me.

"What—" I started. Then I changed it to, "Why?"

"I want all of you, Cora," his said, his eyes shadowed and his voice raspy. "I want to take you in every way. Do you trust me?"

His finger was still there, just barely inside me. I was having a hard time thinking. "Yes. No. I don't know."

"If you want me to stop, tell me now," he ordered.

I shook my head. I couldn't, and he knew it. Whatever it was that he wanted to do to me, I wanted it, too, at least in this moment.

He grasped my leg that was over his shoulder with his free hand, and with the other, I felt three of his fingers spreading me as he began to circle, slowly, with the one inside, pressing down, deeper. It was still wet from me, and it slid inside fractionally deeper with every loop. The sensation was intense, overwhelming. I heard my own breath, catching, whimpering, panting. My body was shaking. Too much—it was too much. And then I felt his knuckle against me, and I realized he was all the way inside. Just then, he pulled out, and I pushed against him reflexively—and he slid back in, so fast that it took my breath away, leaving me gasping.

His erection was above, at my entrance, pushing deep inside so that he filled both places. And he began to thrust, deeply with his erection, shallowly with his hand, until one sensation flowed into the other and it bunched tight in that deep place, knotting harder and harder until it exploded, tearing through me, and I cried out, too loud, desperate, ragged noises that were more animal than human, coming so hard that my head pounded with it, my hands and feet tingling like a hundred wasps had stung them.

And then he shuddered, and I heard him come, too, and it was over. I screwed my eyes shut tight as he pulled away, taking deep, ragged breaths. I kept them shut tight until I heard the sound of the kitchen faucet running, then shut off. I finally looked up to see him drying his hands, his shadowed gaze upon me.

I fled. There was no other word for it. I pushed off the couch and ran into the bathroom, where I shut the door. I turned on the water, got a washcloth, and scrubbed myself, still shuddering with reaction. I didn't know if I was more frightened by what had happened or that I had enjoyed it so much.

CHAPTER NINE

*N*ever, I thought. *Never would I have...*

Where was the line? With Dorian, was there even one? I thought of the woman I'd seen at my introduction, the one with the silvery marks down her back. Would I be like her, too, one day? The idea revolted and fascinated me.

I looked at myself in the mirror, naked except for the necklace at my throat. His necklace.

Even now, I shook with the aftermath of it. I grabbed for the pills on the edge of the pink, popped one out of the foil, and swallowed it, knowing it stopped nothing but needing to do something, anything. Then I closed my eyes, the water still running, and leaned forward to rest my forehead against the cool glass of the mirror.

Geoff would never do that. I was sure of it. Not in a thousand years.

Why did that make me want Dorian all the more?

Taking a steadying breath, I turned off the water. I was spending too much time hiding in bathrooms. I had to make a choice. Soon. I was afraid that it might already be too late.

I stepped out of the bathroom—and back into Dorian's arms. He kissed me, slowly, lingeringly, thoroughly, until my head was swimming and I was ready to surrender to him all over again.

"I wasn't thinking," he said when he finally pulled back. His hands were tight, too tight, on my shoulders. "I'm sorry, Cora. I like to flatter myself that by now...." He broke off and pulled me against his bare chest again.

And I felt at home there. Even after everything, even with all my fears, it felt so right. I wondered how I'd ever lived without knowing the smell of his skin. I didn't know where he'd been going with that sentence, and I didn't care—I, who always cared too much, who was always afraid that I wasn't doing the right thing—I just didn't care.

He loosened his hold on me—gradually, as if reluctantly. He caressed my cheek, his eyes so deep I thought I could lose myself in them. He looked like he was about to speak, but even as his lips parted, he shook his head.

Instead, he said, "Say the word. If ever you want me to stop, I will. I promise, Cora."

"I don't think I can," I said. "I don't know if I'll be

able to want you to stop. Ever."

"I will keep you safe." The words carried the weight of a vow. "Even from yourself."

I took a shaky breath. Safe. Dorian was the exact opposite of safe.

But all I said was, "Let me change and pack an overnight bag, okay?"

"Sure," he said, and he stepped back far enough that my beating heart could return to its normal pace, and the world returned to some semblance of its steady state.

I ducked into the bedroom and pulled on some clean clothes, then grabbed my duffel and stuffed it with my toiletries, picture, laptop, and my stuffed rabbit Nibbler. I went back into the bathroom and got my pills and shoved them into the outer pocket. My hand hovered over my toothbrush and toothpaste, but I decided to leave them this time. For some reason, I didn't mind using the ones Dorian had provided. It wasn't the same as wearing his clothes.

Or his necklace? I thought. But I pushed that aside.

When I came back into the living area, Dorian was lounging against the back of the kitchen peninsula, wearing the remains of his shirt under his suit coat. He looked perfectly at ease—until I looked at his hands, which were gripping the edge of the counter tightly enough to make his knuckles white.

"I'm ready," I said. "Let's go."

I found my keys on the kitchen counter and led the way out. I avoided his gaze in the elevator, remembering too keenly how his body had felt against mine, pushing me hard into the corner, that corner, wanting him to do it again....

I was glad to escape into the crisp night air. The bite of it cooled my flaming cheeks. I put my head down and walked next to him toward his car. He held the door open for me, and I mumbled a "thank you" as I took my seat, tossing my bag in the back.

He broke the silence as he backed out of the parking space. "I called while you were dressing. Dinner will be ready when we arrive."

I looked at the dashboard. It was already 6:30. "Thanks," I said.

"Unless you want to eat in a more public setting," he added, the words careful, studied.

"Unless you scared me that much, you mean." I wished that he had. My choice would have been much simpler then. "No. It's fine. I'm okay."

"I want you to be more than okay," he said. His eyes were locked on the view through the windshield. "It's been a very long time for me, since I've had...this. I hadn't intended...." He gave a laugh. "Anything. I didn't plan. I always plan."

Dorian sounded amazed, almost bewildered. I looked sharply at him. Of all the things I'd expected from him, confusion wasn't one of them. I was always the one to be confused, torn, battered—and powerless in the grip of his certainty.

Now that he didn't have that certainly, I was lost at sea. I couldn't even think of anything to say. What was there that I *could* say? The cracks that I had seen the night of the introduction, they had deepened, and now the mask was falling away. And I was no less frightened of what I'd find underneath.

Frightened that it would bind me even closer to him.

"Whatever happens, understand that you never need to fear me, Cora," Dorian said. "I won't let you be truly hurt."

I rubbed my wrist where he had drunk from me. Nothing that wouldn't quickly heal, he meant. The image of the woman's back rose again in my mind, crisscrossed with layered scars, and I shuddered.

"Do you want to?" I asked. "Truly hurt me."

Dorian was silent for a very long time, so long that I began to wonder if maybe I'd only thought that I said the words aloud.

Finally, he spoke. "We are demonspawn, Cora. Some impulses are not to be indulged. Ever. With anyone."

My lungs felt suddenly tight. My own monster. A monster with a conscience, a moral code that he had forged out of...what? Vampires apparently didn't get prophets or books from God. That meant they had to borrow their ideals...from us.

I thought of how terrible humans could be. My stomach clenched.

"I met a woman at your Lesser Introduction," I said, not realizing that I was going to tell him until the words were out of my mouth. "She was the reason you found me at the other end of the ballroom—because she frightened me, I mean. A cognate. She was covered in these marks." I held up my forearm where the silvery lines left where his teeth had cut the skin stood out in the streetlights. "Everywhere. All over her body."

Dorian looked at my arm, and his face went hard. "Lucretia. It's no wonder she succeeded in terrorizing you."

"You know who I'm talking about?" I asked.

He snorted. "Everyone knows Lucretia. She makes sure of that. She's Cosimo Laurentis' cognate, and for sheer spite and horribleness, she would be a close second to Veronica only because there is only so much damage a cognate could do on her own."

"Cosimo?" I blurted.

"You've met him?" The question was as sharp as a whiplash.

"I...yes...." Suddenly, that night took on an entirely new context. Lucretia, sent to frighten me into Cosimo's waiting arms, to prepare me for his message of escape....

"I'm so stupid," I blurted. "Oh, my God, he planned it all along—"

"Planned what?" Dorian demanded, his hands tightening on the steering wheel.

"Lucretia scared me, and I ran for the stairs. Cosimo stopped me, talked me into staying, and then left me where you found me later...."

Cosimo had positioned me next to the rushers on purpose, abandoning me where I would, at the least, be a witness to an ugly scene. And if that hadn't frightened me enough, he'd planned the field trip to The Plant to top it off. All so that I'd be eager to listen when he told me how a bond could be broken.

And I'd sat in the car next to him, just inches away from an agnate who had layered abuse after abuse on his cognate's body. He's touched me with the same hands that had done that to her, smiled at me, pretended concern, pretended even to be my friend.

"Stay away from him," Dorian ordered. "He's dangerous. And he is most definitely not on our side."

"I thought it was a coincidence," I said. "I should have realized—"

"No." Dorian cut me off. "You didn't know any better. It was my job to protect you. I didn't do as well as I should."

"You keep secrets," I said, thinking of what Cosimo had said about breaking bonds. "How can I stay safe with all your secrets?"

He ran a hand through his hair—a rare response that I'd come to associate with tightly controlled frustration. "They aren't secrets, Cora. You have an entirely new society—a new biology—to take in, and on top of that, a thousand years of rivalries to understand. You've only been conscious of this world for a week. These things take time—to learn and to understand, both."

"But if there's a danger now, I need to know," I objected. "I need to know everything."

I need you to tell me about this bond-breaking. I need to hear it from your lips. And then, maybe I can begin to trust....

"And you will. In due course," he said.

I made a noise of irritation, scowling at his patrician profile. "I'm not your possession to do whatever you want with," I said. "I deserve answers now, not when you think it'll be best for me. Don't tell me it's for my own good. You don't get to make that decision."

"I think that my experience and position in this world would give me some judgment on this matter," he countered, suddenly cold.

"If I accept that reason for you protecting me or hiding things from me or coddling me, then it'll never have an end. You can say that as easily a century from now—that your experience is far vaster than my own, that your knowledge is greater than what I can have built in my insignificant life. Whether or not it's true doesn't matter. I can't live like that."

His mouth was hard. "What do you want? A course book? I'm telling you things as fast as I know how."

"No, you're not," I said. "I asked you how vampires are born, and you refused point blank to tell me."

"Because you weren't ready to know," he said.

"That's not your decision to make," I said again.

His knuckles went white on the steering wheel. "You have no idea how hard you make this for me."

"It won't get easier," I said. "Not with me."

"What did you want me to say, then? Did you want me to lay out the entire socio-political landscape for you? How many years of study do you have?" he demanded. "Even now, you barely understand. Do you think Veronica's ambitions extend no farther than self-gratification? That's not why she bears children as fast as she possibly can."

I remembered the agnate from the introduction, her belly swollen with pregnancy.

Dorian continued, "She's breeding an army, and until now, the Kyrioi have been able to handily outproduce us. Their goal is the subjugation of humankind under an agnatic world order, in which all humans are reduced to a state of serfdom with no purpose other than to enrich their betters."

The words were ugly. I hated Dorian's world—hated its brutality and its demands. "And I'm supposed to—to outbreed *her*. I'm supposed to live a thousand years. Save four thousand humans from death at your hands. And bear you soldiers for your cause. More vampires, who will kill more humans. When does it stop?"

"When we find the perfect test and no more humans must die." Dorian's voice sounded weary.

He didn't have a right to be tired of this argument. It was my future that he was talking about—the future that he required of me. "That's what I am to you, isn't it? Your baby-maker. All the rest of this—it's just trappings. It's the drug that keeps me hooked on you, so I'll do what you want."

"No." He didn't raise his voice, but all his power was in that single word, rocking me in my seat. "Not unless you're my drug, too."

My head was pounding. He was the agnate, the master of this bond. I was its victim. Wasn't he?

Wasn't I?

"Why do you insist on seeing evil where there is none?" he continued.

"No evil?" I protested. "Agnates kill people, Dorian. You can't get around that."

"Was it evil for me to give you a chance at life when you had none?" he asked. "Knowing everything, would you choose death by cancer over a chance of life with me?"

"You know I couldn't," I said. "I want to live." But which life? My old one, with all its possibilities—or my new one, which must revolve completely around him?

"There are thousands of others dying every day who would take the same gamble," Dorian said. "Would you deny them healing?"

I shook my head.

"Every Adelphoi will be able to offer other humans at least the same chance you had," he pressed on. "If you accepted it, it can't be evil."

"I don't want my children to kill," I said.

"Maybe they won't have to, by that point. And maybe we'll discover other ways to help people live."

"Other ways?"

"Perfecting the test is only the first step. There's so much we don't understand about the process of conversion. If we could at least harness some part of that and, for example, create an injection that converts cancerous cells back into a noncancerous form, or repairs the marrow where misshapen blood cells are produced in sickle-cell anemia, or even repairs more fundamental DNA errors—"

I'd stopped listening at the first item in his list. "You could cure cancer."

"We could cure all genetic disease, too, and so much more," Dorian said. "There are two possible futures, Cora, and one of them will happen, whether or not you want them to. In both, there will be agnates, and we will either live peacefully alongside humans and even help them as we are able, or we will live as their masters."

And I would be living in one of those worlds, whether or not I was with Dorian. If I went back to my ordinary life, my human life, everything that he was working for would still happen—or else everything he feared. I could choose to be ignorant, and I could choose to not play a role. But I couldn't stop it from happening.

"What would you have done if I had told you all this on the first day?" he said.

"I don't know." I didn't know what I'd do now. "If this is all so important, so much bigger than us, why aren't you making sure that I can't screw it up?"

"You mean by turning you into an Isabella." He was silent for a long moment, and in the flickering streetlights, I saw an internal struggle play briefly across his face. "There are two answers, the political and the personal."

"Okay," I said. "Tell me, then."

"Politically, you're not just a symbol for the success of my research. You're a symbol for everything we stand for—respect for humans and respect for cognates."

"That's a big gamble," I said. "If you fail—"

"If *we* fail. You're with us now, Cora. And I believe—I must believe—that you won't let all this be destroyed."

CHAPTER TEN

Dorian knew. He had to know what I had almost done the night before. He must have felt it, like he felt my grief.

And he hadn't come after me. He could have tried to come, tried to arrive in time to stop me. But he didn't.

Why did he trust me? Did he really believe in me? Or in the bond? Or in what he'd done to me through it? If he wanted me as badly as he claimed, he had the power to make it so that he never, ever had to let me go....

"And there is the other reason," he continued, breaking into those thoughts. "The personal one." He didn't look at me, and the pitch of his voice didn't change, but the conviction in those words made me swallow hard. "I'd hurt you, even though you wouldn't know that you were hurt—break what you are now, forever. I couldn't do that to you, Cora."

"What about your ideals?" I challenged. "What if it's the higher good to scramble me around until I didn't know whether I was coming or going? What if you were convinced it was the only right thing to do?"

"It isn't." His jaw tightened.

"But what if it was?"

He was silent for a long moment, and then he said, heavily, "I don't know."

I shivered. "What should I make of you, Dorian?"

"Falling angel or ascending demon?" he offered. He smiled ever so slightly, but his eyes were sad when they finally met mine.

I nodded, not quite trusting myself to speak.

"Perhaps a little of both."

I lifted one shoulder. "That's what I'm afraid of."

He had nothing to say to that.

Dorian pulled down a street a block short of his house. I frowned, but then I saw the familiar holly hedge on either side of a wide, arched garage door, and I realized that his property extended the entire depth of the block. The door opened at the touch of a button, and he drove in.

The floor sloped steeply, and then the room opened up on either side to reveal a vast subterranean garage containing a mind-boggling fleet of cars. The floor was tiled in black and white, the room lit by recessed lights that flicked on automatically as we entered.

"Jay Leno would be jealous," I said lightly, changing the subject as he pulled into an empty parking space.

"As I mentioned before, I collect cars," he said, and this time his smile reached his eyes.

"Where are we now?" I asked. "Under the house?"

"Under the garden," he said. He unbuckled and turned off the car. "Coming?"

"Right behind you," I said, ducking out of the passenger door.

He met me on the passenger's side of the car. Catching me with one arm, he pulled me in to him. In spite of everything, I tilted back my head for his kiss, thorough and expert, waking the half-banked fires inside me.

"I want you to be happy with me, Cora," he murmured into my hair.

"I'm afraid," I admitted. "I'm afraid that I can be. I'm not sure I should."

He held me against his side as he led me to a door in the wall of the garage. Beyond it, the floor turned from tile to wide slabs of granite, with matching walls. The great arches above reminded me of my dream, those many weeks before.

"Where are we now?"

"The cellars," he said.

"What's down here?" I asked as we passed by tightly shut wooden doors.

"Wine cellar. Cheese cellar. Coal and furnace room, which I had converted to a boiler and general mechanical room some time ago. Scullery. Larder, though now of course there's a proper fridge and freezer. And the laboratory, with the clean rooms for research."

"So your research actually is being done here? I mean, in your house?"

"It's safest to keep it near," he said.

I had a sense of being hidden in the wings as crucially important things were happening all around me. Or under my feet, as was the case with the research lab that had decided my fate without my ever having interacted with a single staff member responsible for the test that sealed my future.

"Do you really trust me, Dorian?" I asked as we reached a flight of stairs.

"I must," he said.

But he didn't really have to, not the way I had to trust him. At any moment, he could change me, wipe me clean, as Isabella had been wiped. All that stopped him was a promise. I rubbed the new silvery marks on my arm. Or he could turn me into his toy, like Lucretia. And I would be powerless to stop him. I was very much afraid that I might want him to.

"That's why I want to show you something else down here," he continued. He guided me down a short hallway with more nondescript doors. He stopped in front of a blank section of wall. No, it wasn't blank, after all. There was the shape of a doorway, but it was bricked over with stone in a slightly different color, all except for a narrow slot about three inches high and a foot wide.

My stomach felt suddenly uneasy.

"What is this?" I asked.

"Alys' room," he said. "And now her tomb."

CHAPTER ELEVEN

I recoiled but was brought up short when I ran into Dorian's chest.

"Who was she?" I managed to ask, backing quickly away. Some dire foe? Some would-be assassin? Some ex-cognate who had rejected him?

"One of my oldest friends," he said heavily. "The closest thing I had to a sister. A casualty in this war of ours. She couldn't stand the killing anymore, couldn't stand the human waste, but she knew that she wouldn't be able to stop herself, eventually, from feeding when the urge got strong enough. Madness would set in, eventually irreversible, and she, like all of us, would become the monster you name us in truth. No longer a thinking, rational creature—just a beast, who knows nothing but hunger and is never full."

The full horror of what I was looking at came upon me. "So you bricked her up in there. Alive."

Dorian reached out and placed his palm flat against the bricks, his shoulders bowed as if under a great weight. "Alive and sane, at her request. She was determined to take her own life by more immediate means if I would not agree to it."

"But this amounted to the same thing, didn't it?" I asked.

"It was not suicide," he said—almost angrily. More calmly, he added, "Not exactly. Her death was the inevitable result of her choice to kill no more, but it was not her main aim. For three months, she took food and water through the door. I talked to her daily—pleaded with her at first to change her mind, told her that the test was getting better every month, that if she just kept the faith for a while longer, we could all be free. But she said, 'Not at the cost of another life.'"

"God, Dorian," I said. I wondered if I could be so noble. I thought of how desperate I'd been to live, and I wasn't sure I had it in me.

But he didn't even seem to see me anymore, staring at the mute, cold wall as if he were telling it its own history. "Our conversations changed as she lost herself gradually. The wit and humor that I'd so loved about her went first. Reason followed, and for a while, she babbled nonsense when I tried to speak to her. And then speech went altogether. She stopped eating, stopped drinking, and made noises like an animal in mortal pain."

The hand against the wall turned into a fist. "I wanted to let her out so badly. But there was nothing of my Alys left in her, then, and I would have been releasing a monster that I would have then been forced to put down, if it did not overcome me. So instead, I sat here against the wall and waited for her to die. For three long weeks, I waited for her to die. And when she did, I left her there, behind this damned wall, because I knew she didn't want me to see what she had become."

And then he hauled back his fist and hit the wall with such force that the sound struck my ears like another blow, and a web of cracks spidered out from where his flesh met the brick.

I jumped back reflexively—then forward again, because when he dropped his hand, his knuckles were covered in his blood.

"Dorian," I said, a protest in his name as I stepped forward to grab his hand. By the time I'd wiped his knuckles with the tail of my shirt to assess the damage, his skin was whole again, nothing but the faintest marks betraying what he'd done, already fading in front of my eyes.

I looked up at him, tried to see the seeds of a mad beast behind his grieving eyes. I could too well imagine him sitting there, listening to her noises grow fainter, knowing that he had the same creature inside himself. Man and monster.

And I understood for the first time what this fight meant for him in the personal sense rather than in the greater abstraction of evil and good.

"We have to win, Cora," he said, turning his wrist

in my grip so that he held my hands in his. "We must. This can't all be for nothing."

"It won't." I made the promise before I realized I was going to say anything at all.

He took a deep, shuddering breath, and the sadness disappeared as if a curtain had been pulled over his face.

"Come, now," he urged. "Dinner is waiting."

And not knowing what else to do, I let him guide me up out of the cellars into the main part of the house. Dinner was laid out for us at a small table in his bedroom, every detail carefully attended to, as always. As we ate, I struggled to make small talk, but the weight of Dorian's revelations was too great for me.

My world had been so simple, so straightforward. When I looked into my future, it encompassed my job, my family, my friends. I wanted to make my Gramma proud, but nothing else depended on me. Certainly not the future of humanity.

"I'm sorry," I said abruptly, breaking into Dorian's answer to my question about the landscape painting over his fireplace.

He stopped and looked at me across the table. "Yes?"

"I...I think I may have been selfish," I said.

"In what way?" he asked carefully.

I made a face involuntarily. Some part of me had wished that he'd flatly contradict me. But that wasn't in Dorian's nature. So I answered his question.

"You want this," I said, making a motion to indicate him, me, everything. "And I've been pretty hung up on that, that you chose it and I didn't. But you want this at least partly because of the bigger thing you want—winning, I mean, not just for you but because it's so important to everybody, everything."

I realized I was babbling, and I tried to clarify. "When you do what you need to so that you'll win, you don't really have that many choices. I mean, you had one big choice, to be an Adelphoi, but once you made that choice, you had to do all the things that that one big choice meant. It locks you into a path. Am I making any sense at all?"

Dorian raised an eyebrow. "Perfectly."

"I want all my choices, though," I continued. "I can't really have them all. But I want them anyway. And I don't think I can make just one big choice, like you can. I have to make the little ones—the ones for me."

"We all start somewhere, Cora," he said.

That should have irritated me. It was terribly condescending, wasn't it? To him, well, maybe there had been a similar start at some point in the distant past. Maybe it was only his intangible ideals that stood between him and the darkness within. But where did that leave me?

I was still just an ordinary college student with ordinary dreams and ambitions. I had to be, or else I might become someone my Gramma didn't know. If I changed too much, strayed too much from how she'd seen me, it'd be like losing her all over again, or maybe like she'd lose me.

Suddenly, I rebelled from that, rebelled from everything. Here I was, telling Dorian that I had to make my decisions for myself, that I couldn't consider myself as just another tool in the Adelphoi's goals, and not a minute later, I was thinking of myself in the terms of what my grandmother wanted for me. Not what I wanted for myself. I'd thrown myself into her vision of a perfect life, embraced it as my own dream, but was it?

I thought of Geoff. I liked him a lot. Almost loved him, just a little. And I loved the college student life, not because Gramma wanted me to but for myself. All that was good.

And yet when I dug down deep, into my heart, there was a seed that wasn't my own—my grandmother's determination that my life would be happy in a certain way.

What if I chose a life that was happy in another way? Would she really reject it because it had no resemblance to the happy picture she'd kept so sacred in her mind?

And, I thought brutally, should I change my life just because she might? If I was choosing for myself, I had to choose completely for myself, one way or another. Not for her.

I looked at Dorian, idly twirling a fork as he watched me finish dinner. He still wore the gaping shirt missing the buttons that he'd pulled off. I realized that I was tired of being acted on. I was tired of responding. And I was damned tired of being everybody's pawn. It was my turn to act, to decide, to take charge.

I still didn't know what I wanted for myself tomorrow, much less in five years or ten. But right now, at that moment, I wanted Dorian.

And I would have him.

I pushed back from the table and stood up, and he instantly rose, too—some kind of chivalrous reflex that didn't allow him to sit when there was a woman standing in the room. I circled around to him and stopped. Whatever my expression was, my intent must have been clear because his eyes went shadowed and he caught the back of my neck and pulled me to his lips.

I let myself get lost in his kiss for a long moment, his mouth hot and hungry on my own. But then I pulled back.

"No," I said. "This time, it's my turn."

I reached for his belt. He closed his hands over mine, but I looked up at him.

"Let me do this, Dorian."

He let go, standing with his feet planted while his gaze roved across my body, devouring me.

My turn. My turn to act, my turn to decide, my turn to choose—and right now, I chose him, I chose this, the one act that I could do to him in which I was in complete and utter control.

A little astonished at myself—not at what I was going to do but that I was going to do it to him, to Dorian, the powerful vampire—I loosened his belt, then the zipper and the button beneath. I pushed his pants over his hips, sliding them down. I was confronted by his boxer briefs, the bulge of his hardness already stretching the fabric. I slid them down, too. His erection sprang away from his body as the fabric cleared the head. I reached down and took it in my hand, making a circle with my fingers around the shaft.

It was faintly warm, which surprised me, because

Dorian's skin was almost always cool to the touch, even in the throes of passion. His skin was oddly velvety, soft over the hardness beneath. I moved my hand slowly, experimentally, the skin moving over it with each stroke.

"You've never done this before," Dorian said, his voice strained. It was not a question.

"No," I said. I stopped, suddenly overcome with self-doubt. "It isn't bad, is it?"

He gave a ragged kind of laugh. "I promise, Cora, with you, bad is an impossibility."

Impossible for him as it was for me? That was a revelation.

I wondered what I could do to him, if I could fill up his world with nothing but pleasure and his awareness of me, the way he could to me. That thought made me suddenly greedy. I wanted him to give me every bit as much of himself as he took from me.

Eagerly now, I began to move my hand up and down again, sliding the skin over the shaft and head. His fingers closed over mine for a moment, urging a firmer grip, so I did. Up and down I stroked him, biting my lip, my eyes fixed on the wetness that began to glisten at the tip. I wanted to see his need in his face, but I couldn't look away from it.

I felt a small shudder go through his frame, and my own breathing sped up. I felt heat bloom between my legs, and I kept my eyes on my hands and his hard cock.

I stopped, let go.

"Sit down," I ordered. I ordered him—Dorian. The rush of it went to my head and down between my legs.

Dorian pulled off his shoes and pushed his pants

the rest of the way off, leaving them on a pile on the floor so that he was naked from the waist down. Then he took two steps back to the chair he had left and sat, turning it to face me.

I looked up then, and my heart and stomach jumped at what I saw in his face, a need so intense that it looked like pain. He needed me. I'd done that to him. And I was going to do more.

I knelt slowly between his knees. His erection—no, not his erection, it was too earthy and vital a thing for such a word—his dick, his cock—it was just inches away now. I felt a kind of giddy, reckless excitement rush through me.

My hands encircled the girth of him again, holding it steady. I bent down and took the head into my mouth. I saw his thigh muscles flex, go rigid as I surrounded it. It was smooth against my tongue, salty and slightly musky. And I loved the taste of him even as I loved the tightening of his legs and the way his hands went rigid on the arms of the chair.

I cushioned my teeth with my lips. Slowly, I slid it deeper, farther into my mouth, and then I began working up and down, stroking him with my tongue, sucking against the rounded head.

I could hear his breath hissing through his teeth, and I knew I was doing to him what he had done to me so many times before. I was filling his brain with it, with his desire for me, until there wasn't room for anything else. I watched him as I worked him, up and down. His head was thrown back, the Adam's apple of his throat standing out against the taut muscles of his strong neck.

He was so beautiful like that, so perfect even in the throes of his pleasure, and it was me making his whole body go stiff and his throat move as he struggled to even swallow as his breath grew louder in my ears, small, deep noises at the catching start of every breath.

"Cora—" he said, and there was a warning in his voice.

But I didn't stop, I didn't slow, even as one of his hands found my hair and tightened in it. I knew what was going to happen, and I wouldn't be satisfied until it did—until I'd taken that from him, as he'd taken it from me so many times.

My jaw was aching slightly from accommodating him, but even that gave me a strange thrill. Up and down I moved, breathing with it, sucking him, my hands and mouth working together.

Suddenly, he let out a deep groan, and as he did, the tip of his erection exploded into my mouth, pulsing. As the taste of him filled me, I took it as my victory. Then I pulled away and, rather inelegantly, wiped it onto the tail of my shirt.

Dorian laughed, a little breathlessly. "Bad?"

"No," I said, and I thought, *Mine.* He was mine, his pleasure was mine, his orgasm was mine, even his cum—yes, that, even in its crudest word, that was mine, too. I met his gaze boldly. "How was it for you?"

I knew how it was. Every line of his body had told me. But I wanted to hear his words—I wanted to make them mine, too.

"Very good," he said, his voice rough with reaction. "Very, very good, indeed." His eyes glinted with a light that made my breath hitch. "And now, I believe I owe you."

Chapter Twelve

I laughed, lightheaded. "I think the debt is still in your favor at the moment."

"Be that as it may, even though I'm an agnate, I am not up for another go quite yet," Dorian said, his eyes hooded even as he smiled down at me. "But you... Women—of all races—are different. For you, there is no arbitrary limit."

"Limit?" I asked as I rocked back on my heels, pretending coyness even as my heart began to thrum in my ears. "What do you mean by that?"

He leaned down, bringing his face close to mine. "If I keep you right at the edge, I could keep you coming all night long."

"How?" I demanded, a little amazed at my own audacity because I knew I was challenging him, and I didn't doubt that he could do exactly what he said.

"Do you trust me?" he asked.

"I don't know that I should," I said.

He gave me a slow, languorous smile that liquefied my insides.

"But I think I'd like to try," I added, giving into recklessness again.

He stood and looked down at me. "Then the first order of business is to get you out of those clothes."

Oh, yes, I agreed silently. *Let's do that.*

Dorian stood and pulled me to my feet to meet him, his arms coming around me as his mouth found mine. His kiss was slow, methodical, and complete, plundering my mouth with dizzying deftness as he stroked me with his tongue.

He drove me back toward the bed. I offered no resistance—because I chose not to, not because I couldn't. This was the game right now, and I wanted to play it. I felt the mattress against the back of my thighs, and then his hands were under my rear, and he broke the kiss as he boosted me up and tossed me lightly onto my back into the center of the bedspread.

I giggled despite myself and began wiggling to turn parallel to the headboard, but he said, "Don't move."

I froze, and he lay down next to me, resuming the kiss as my head flooded with hot need and my center began to send little throbs down between my legs.

Dorian lifted my shirt a mere inch and moved down to kiss my stomach where it was exposed. It should have tickled, but instead, it drove another shivering spike through me. He moved up slowly, his mouth staking claim to every inch that his hands exposed until the shirt was at my neck. He pulled it off then, tossing it to the ground, and moved to my bra.

This time, he didn't unhook it, instead kissing along the arc formed by the underwire as he pushed it up, millimeter by millimeter, over my breasts. I was shaking by the time his mouth began working against my areola, shamelessly rocking my hips into his hard thigh. I felt the underwire pull up against my hard nipples, stretching them fractionally as his lips and teeth teased the lower edge...then they pulled free, and I moaned as his mouth found them, still blocked by the edge of the bra from forming the suction I craved. And up the bra went, up a little more, and then he was fully over them, his mouth and hands stroking, pulling, teasing them until I was mad with it all.

"Please," I begged squirming against him, "please."

The suckling suddenly turned into a sharp bite, and I gasped, feeling it all the way down into my clit. Oh, it hurt, hurt so good, as only Dorian could make me feel....

He released me, and then he was pulling off my bra, over my head. I lifted my arms to free them, then slid one hand brazenly down into my pants, finding the hard, swollen nub of my clitoris—

"Oh, no, you don't," Dorian said, capturing my hand. "Not tonight."

He let go of me and pulled away abruptly. I sat up, dazed, just in time to see him disappear through the door that led to his dressing room.

"Dorian?" I called. Had I offended him somehow?

I was baffled, dazed, throbbing with unfulfilled need—

Just as I was about to roll off the bed to find him, he reappeared in the doorway holding a gold silk cord. I recognized it as the tie to his smoking jacket.

My heart sped up. "I'm not so sure—" I began.

"Did you like it when you wore the corset and I made you come so hard you couldn't breathe?" he asked bluntly.

Wordlessly, I nodded.

"This is much the same idea." He reached the bed. "A loss of control."

"I never feel in control with you," I said shakily.

His smile was predatory. "Good. Now, wrists."

There was no compulsion in those words, no more than the ordinary force of will that he wore around him like a dark cloak, but I held out my hands, wrists together. He bound them together, the silk cutting a little into my skin.

"And up," he said, and he scooped me up and deposited me closer to the head of the bed.

I opened my mouth, but before I could speak, he was pushing me back into the pillows as he lifted my hands over my head. I tilted my head back and watched him tie the ends of the cords to the closest bedpost, so that I was stretched out on the bed with my breasts bare and vulnerable to him.

"And now it's my turn," he said, lowering himself between my legs.

He turned his attention to the flesh that he had already bared, moving over my mouth, my neck, my breasts, my belly, sucking them, nipping them, then kissing away the tiny bee-stings of pain. I whimpered, trying to bring my hands down, to cling to him or guide him or shield my body from the dizzying onslaught, I didn't know, but the bindings only cut harder into my skin.

Then he moved to the button of my jeans, and I braced myself, knowing what was coming next. He twisted it open, then kissed it for a long moment, his fingers digging into my butt, before he slid the zipper down, a fraction of an inch at a time, his fingers hooked in my underwear and drawing them with it.

When he reached the end of the zipper, he lingered there, his mouth in my curls, so close to my aching clitoris that I bit my lip against my pleas until I tasted a tang of blood.

His hands slipped under my waistband and pulled, slowly, too slowly, until the top of my pants was bunched below my hips. And then, only then, did his mouth find the tight, aching place, coming full against my clitoris and tearing a grateful cry from my throat.

Sensation swirled up through me as I jerked down against the cords that held me tight, and I came against his mouth, rocking my hips into it, needing even more even as the orgasm shook through me.

"That is only the beginning," he said, and he pulled my pants lower still, to my knees, so that he could kiss and nip the insides of my thighs—and then, oh yes, then, he licked me hard from the base of my entrance all the way to my clitoris. And then, somehow, he was pressing against it, rocking it even as his tongue pushed between the folds at the top of my opening, and one of his hands slid up from cradling my butt to slide into my entrance just behind it and pull down, stretching me as I clenched hard against him.

I was still at the edge, and that tipped me over again, into the heat that buzzed through my body. My clit throbbed, my nipples, my lips, my anus—everything buzzed and crackled with it, and when it dissipated, I was left breathless, raw, and whimpering.

"I have something for you." It was Dorian's voice, a velvety, dangerous caress. "Do you think you're ready?"

I shook my head, then nodded, afraid of what he could mean but craving it, nevertheless.

He extended his body over mine, leaning over to the bedside table. He pulled open a drawer, then extracted a small case, which he opened.

I could make no sense of what lay on the silk-lined interior. They looked rather like three alligator clips, except that they were shorter and had no teeth, and they were joined together with a Y-shaped chain.

"You like how it feels when my mouth is on your nipples, your clit," he said. It was not a question.

"Oh," I said, my eyes widening instinctively as I understood what these were for.

"Yes," he agreed, looking down at me with a glittering gaze.

My breath came fast as I realized that I couldn't stop him from using those on me even if I wanted to, not with my arms tied helplessly above my head. I shook my head, trying to decide, among my warring feelings, which was the strongest—which the uppermost. I couldn't.

"Tell me no, Cora," Dorian said. "Tell me no, and I'll put them away."

I could hear the tension in his voice—how much he wanted to use these on me. And I wanted it, too, though I was more than half afraid that it was another step into the darkness from which I would never return.

"When?" I asked, not looking away from them. "When did you get these?"

"Christmas Eve," he said.

After the first time we'd slept together. He'd gotten them for me. I should be horrified. I should be horrified and disgusted and afraid....

But I wasn't.

"I want you to do it." I barely recognized my own voice, strained and high. "Do it."

"First, I must make you ready again," he said, and his mouth found mine.

The kiss started slowly, but then it grew harder, almost frantic. He tongue all but attacked me, his teeth nipping at my lip. I gasped under the onslaught, staggered. When he pulled away, he was shaking.

"Oh, God, Cora, blood," he said. "What are you trying to do to me?"

"I—I don't know," I said, yearning for him and frightened at the same time.

His eyes burned. "I will not go too far," he said, and for a moment, I wondered if he was trying to convince himself or me.

But I had no time to think about that, because then he was kissing me again, on the throat, the collarbone, across the top curve of my breast until he found one nipple and teased it, hard, until I cried out with the throbbing ripples that it sent through my body. His mouth lifted, and then something cold and hard slipped around it and squeezed so that echoes of the pleasure continued to reverberate through my body.

I shuddered, hardly noticing that his mouth was moving on until it closed over my other breast, and he repeated the action. This time, the reaction was intensified by the unrelenting pressure on my other breast, and I moaned and writhed against him until he pulled away, slipping the other clamp over the nipple as his mouth left it.

He pulled back and looked at me for a long moment. I lay there, tugging futilely on the cords, aching to touch myself as the clamps continued to send shivering reactions through my body.

"Do something," I pleaded.

And he did, though not what I had expected. His hand went down between my legs, two fingers pushing inside of me, finding that place again and pressing rhythmically into it as his mouth returned to my swollen nipples, his tongue and teeth teasing, rasping the exposed tips that stuck out above the metal bands.

It was terrible and wonderful, too much and yet not nearly enough as the place deep inside me ached with emptiness. But I peaked again, shattering, mindless, and I felt the throbbing of my blood against the clamps, in my head, down in my clit and in that place where his fingers pressed, pressed me onward, my pants still tangled around my knees, my arms yanking uselessly at the unforgiving cords.

And then he was tugging, pulling at the chain as I rocked with my orgasm, sending me deeper into it, whether with pain or pleasure, I couldn't tell.

Finally, it receded, and I was almost weeping with the force of it, so much that my brain defied me to take it all in. The fingers inside of me withdrew, sliding over my aching clitoris, and he was kissing me again, softly now, across my arms and neck and belly and legs as I tried to regain my bearings.

He pushed down my pants, pulled them all the way off with the socks and shoes I hadn't even noticed that I was still wearing. They joined my shirt on the floor, and his shirt followed.

"I'm ready now," he said softly as I stared at the ceiling, half in a daze. The compression against my nipples still sent little slivers of sensation shivering through me, keeping me aroused even as my body ached with it. "Are you?"

"I think you could do it," I said. My throat was raw.

"Do what?" he asked.

"Keep me coming all night long. But I don't think you should," I added.

"And why is that?" he asked, a dark humor in his rich voice.

"Because," I said distinctly, "I don't think I'd survive."

He laughed then. "The grand finale, then?"

My blood was already heating again. "Yes," I said. "Definitely, yes."

He kissed me, avoiding my blood-touched mouth, his body over mine as he moved up my throat to the sensitive place just below my ear that made me gasp and grind my hips into him. He slid a hand between us, caught my clitoris and rolled it, teased it in his fingers until it was full and throbbing. Then there came a cold pressure, the third clamp bearing down. And the sensation of the others redoubled as that one joined it.

I whimpered, opening myself to him, needing him to fill me now, *now.*

"Here I am, Cora," he said, and I realized that I had said the last word aloud, a demand and a plea in one. He took my knees, pushed them apart, and my folds opened fully as he thrust into them with force enough to startle the breath from my lungs. My clit and nipples throbbed, and I shook.

"Go," I demanded.

And he did, pushing my knees up almost into my chest as he thrust into me, relentlessly, again and again until I came apart so hard that I lost myself in the searing pleasure of it, a hard black edge that sent me crashing harder into the grip of the climax. I let my mind go, my sight, my hearing, everything except the screaming of my nerves that were overloaded with something like ecstasy and something very much like pain.

I didn't even feel him come, so entrapped was I, and it was only his voice calling my name that brought me out of myself:

"Cora, Cora, oh, God, my Cora," my name like a broken plea on his lips.

And I lay stunned as he stopped, pulled back, and I felt the sudden, tingling release as he removed the clamps from my body.

My vision focused upon him replacing them carefully in their box, and then he tugged for a moment at the knots at my wrists before tearing the cords with two deft movements. They dropped away, and my fingers tingled as the blood rushed back into my hands.

"Well," I said, somewhat stupidly, rubbing my chafed wrists.

He shut the bedside table drawer and he kissed me again, slowly, lingeringly, as if he were trying to speak with his soul through his lips.

"How are you?" he asked when he broke away.

"Good," I managed, as my brain battled to provide fitting superlatives: amazing, terrifying, awesome, mind-blowing, superb, petrifying.

He kissed me one more time, rested his forehead against mine for a long moment, just breathing, the echoes of pain in his eyes as he held me a little too tightly.

"Go to sleep, Cora," he said finally, straightening. "We have a busy day tomorrow."

"Of course," I said. Impulsively, I slid under the covers. He hadn't said whether he meant for me to take my bed or his, but I didn't want to be alone.

He just smiled. "Good night, Cora." He circled to the other side of the bed and reached next to it, flicking off the lights.

"Good night," I said aloud.

I love you.

Oh, shit. My eyes were wide in the darkness. Where had that come from? Was it even true? I didn't know.

I stiffened as I felt him get into the bed next to me. He reached out, found me, and pulled me against his body, his chin resting in my hair.

Did I love him? If so, what did it mean? Not that he gave me pleasure—not that alone. Until that night and his explanation about his struggles, his life, about his lonely vigil as Alys died...I would not have said that I loved him. Wanted him, certainly, needed him, even. But this was different. It was more. Was it really love? Did it matter?

I wasn't sure. I was just afraid that he had ruined me—ruined me for anyone else by driving me further into the dark world of his pleasure that no mortal man could give to me. He was marking me as his alone with his body as surely as he had marked me with his blood the day the bond-mark had been made.

Where did it end, this darkness? What were its limits? And did I dare to find out? Did I even want to, or was that a foolish game of moth and flame?

And what about Geoff and my old life—my real life? I didn't want to let them go, either one. I felt the cage door closing; the arms that gently held me might as well have been iron bands. But I didn't know if I had the strength or will to leave.

Before it was too late.

The story continues in…

BLOOD PRICE

Cora's Choice – Book 6
AETHEREAL BONDS

Want to read the first chapter right now? Sign up for the newsletter at AetherealBonds.com to get exclusive access—for free! Get free content and release updates.

Saved from death by the billionaire vampire Dorian Thorne, Cora Shaw is bound to him, body, mind, and soul. She can free herself from his eternal demands— but only by breaking everything that is between them, forever. Never again will she feel what only he can do to her, never again touch him, speak to him, be with him— and never again must she give her blood or fear her will being overcome by his.

It is a decision that can be made only once. Does she want her old life enough to give up Dorian and his new world? Or is the cost of losing him too high?

Even while she hesitates, there are those who wish to take her choices away all over again.…

ABOUT THE AUTHOR

V. M. Black is the creator of Aethereal Bonds, a sensual paranormal romance urban fantasy series that takes vampires, shifters, and faes where they've never been before. You can find her on AetherealBonds.com. Visit to connect through her mailing list and various social media platforms across the web.

She's a proud geek who lives near Washington, D.C., with her family, and she loves fantasy, romance, science fiction, and historical fiction.

All of her books are available in a number of digital formats. Don't have an e-reader? No problem! You can download free reading apps made by every major retailer from your phone or tablet's app store and carry your books with you wherever you go.